This book is dedicated to my grandmother, who was always an inspiration to me; to my mother, who has always believed in me; and to my amazing wife, whose undying support made this publication dream a reality.

MOONLIGHT

By Damean Mathews

The sun was sinking low to the horizon as Tyler's car entered a large expanse of road, clear on either side, offering a magnificent view of the hazy mountain range that seemed to go to the ends of the earth. A light breeze blew through his open window as he listened to the static buzz from his speakers where two stations battled to take over the frequency he was monitoring. He was used to this interference, knowing that he would soon enter a strong signal zone and classic rock would have dominance once more. He paid little attention as the sound of static grew louder than normal, subconsciously attributing it to the cool atmosphere until a voice broke through.

"Stay in the car. Don't get -," the voice said sternly.

Tyler slowed down a bit, wondering what station he'd picked up. Normally the only stations that were occupying the frequency in this place were his classic rock station and a bluegrass program that he would sometimes catch for a few moments. The static lowered slowly before rising to one more crescendo, allowing him to catch the voice he was almost positive he recognized. The white noise at an almost deafening level, one word came through, driving chills up the young man's back.

"Tyler," the voice said in a soft, almost pleading tone before the static faded to the usual mild din, returning the sound of his two stations dueling for singularity.

There was no doubt in his mind the voice, that he was now almost positive was that of his father, had uttered his name. He drove on, paying little attention to the scenery he'd fallen so in love with since moving to the mountains. He hadn't heard from his father in years, and now his voice was coming in over the radio? How was that possible? Maybe it was some strange high altitude interference and the voice was actually a phone conversation. Perhaps his father had tried to call him and the frequencies had gotten meshed. He'd heard stories before of people hearing cell phone conversations come in over their radio. Granted, that had been when wireless technology was relatively new and he was pretty sure that problem had been fixed, it was the only solution he could come up with. Checking his phone, he saw that he had only one bar and felt that his potential explanation seemed all that much more plausible.

Putting the experience out of his mind as best he could, Tyler drove down the road, once more enjoying the scenery unfolding around him. He'd always enjoyed driving, but he never knew the world could be so beautiful until he moved to Tennessee. Having grown up in Chicago, he hadn't gotten to travel much. With a father who was usually away on business and a mother who typically had her sorrows sufficiently drowned by only the best reds by 8 every night, there wasn't much opportunity for travel. He'd escaped the minute he turned 18, joyriding down the various highways until he'd hit what he now thought of as heaven on Earth. The Great Smoky Mountains had called to him more than he ever thought anything could. From the first glimpse he'd gotten of the jagged, hazy range in the distance he'd known it was the place for him.

The little money he had saved up had allowed him to make use of a condo for about two months while he found work with a local tourist attraction. He didn't think he would ever grow rich being a tour guide, but it put him in a house and paid his bills, allowing him to live a more than comfortable life and be happier than he ever thought possible, not to mention it let him spend 30 hours a week deep in the heart of the mountains with people almost as fascinated by them as he was. The house he lived in was about 15 miles from the small road he normally loved to travel on, which was more of a relief than he cared to admit as he neared his driveway.

Pulling the car onto the cracked, unsealed pavement, he entered his house wearily, suddenly feeling nostalgic for his family. He couldn't suppose he was homesick, because he never felt more at home than he did when he first turned the key in the lock of his house in the Smokies, but he would love to be able to walk into a room and find his parents sitting there together as they so rarely had done. He had only been able to count on them being together three times a year before he hit puberty; Thanksgiving, Christmas Eve and Christmas Day. He seemed to remember a few times they were both around for Halloween and New Year's Eve but didn't have the same certainty he did with the other holidays. As he grew older, the days they actually were home at the same time seemed to diminish to only being those three days, until one year his father didn't come home for Thanksgiving. That was the first time he felt like his parents didn't love each other.

He'd asked his mother where daddy was after he awoke to the scent of fresh pancakes and bacon that year, seeing his father's empty place at the table when he entered the dining room with anticipation. She'd told the young, fragile boy that his father didn't care to come home for this particular holiday, and that they would honestly do just fine without him. Ignoring the tears in her son's eyes she had turned on the famous annual parade, hoping that the oversized balloons would keep him occupied enough for her to begin the family meal. The rest of that day was a blur to Tyler, he realized as he sat on his couch nursing an ice-cold soda and trying to remember when his relationship with his father had collapsed. He supposed the first cracks in their fragile bond appeared on that day, as had those with his mother.

Lost in thought, Tyler began to doze slightly, his hand teetering dangerously with his half-full can of carbonated sugar. As one breath gave way to another, deeper one, his body relaxed more and more until a loud tone brought him back to consciousness with a jolt. Setting his miraculously unspilled drink on the table in front of him, he dove into his pocket to retrieve the phone that was ringing louder with each passing second, seeing the name "Mother" flashing on the screen before putting the warm device to his ear.

"Hey," he said, hoping she wouldn't be in a mood.

"Well hey. I was beginning to think you weren't going to answer."

"I must have dozed off. I just got home a bit ago."

"Long day?"

"Yeah, but I wouldn't have it any other way down here."

"I don't understand how you do the mountains. I never felt comfortable so far away from modern conveniences."

"Modern conveniences? I live in a tourist trap, Mom. We probably have more modern conveniences than you up there in Yankee town."

"Alright, Daniel Boone. Let's call it a tie," she said, laughing as she had when he was young, furthering his nostalgia.

"That's fair for now. But you still have to come see this place. You'll never want to leave."

"I have my doubts. But maybe I'll get there one day."

"I'll hold you to it. What's up," he said, knowing small talk made his mother nervous.

"I just wanted to check on you. I've been a bit uneasy today, for some reason. Is everything OK down there?"

"Yeah, I think so. Well..," he began, contemplating telling her of the incident with the radio, but deciding against it.

"What," she said, a little too eagerly, as if expecting to hear he'd been attacked by a bear and was hopping in the car to come back to the city.

"I just had a weird drive this afternoon. I guess I got a little car sick and homesick. Maybe I need a visit, too."

"You're welcome to come home any time, Tyler. You know that, right?"

"Yeah, Mom. I know. But this is my home now. I don't know how to describe it, but I feel like I belong here."

"I know what you mean. Once you find something that makes you feel that way, it's hard to let go. I would never ask you to do that."

"I know," he said, wondering where exactly her sentimentality was coming from.

"I just needed to check on you. I'll let you go for tonight. Just be safe, OK?"

"Of course, Mom. I'm always safe."

"Good. I love you. And Tyler," she said, an exceedingly odd tone in her voice.

"Yeah, Mom?"

"Don't get yourself into any trouble down there, OK?"

"Of course not. I love you, Mom. Have a good night."

Tyler wandered into the kitchen after his mother said her goodbye, still pondering over why she'd been acting so strange. The odd radio interference had all but left his mind for this new occurrence that seemed even more out of place. Typically, conversations with her went more along the lines of her trying to bully him or guilt him back home. She'd fallen into a deep depression when he left, he knew, and hadn't been able to fully recover from the negative effect it had had on both of them. For her to be suddenly so warm, welcoming, and accepting put him in a defensive mode that even he didn't recognize.

He pulled a thin steak from his refrigerator and threw it in a pan, finally feeling the pangs of hunger that he knew should be more prominent than they were. As the meat began to sizzle, the scent filling the small kitchen, Tyler felt his hunger reach an all new high. He turned up his can and finished the sugary drink inside, already feeling like he could use another. In no time the steak was done to his preference. Slapping it between two pieces of bread and choosing a glass of milk over another soda, he sat in front of the television and prepared to immerse himself in his favorite Monday night shows.

The rest of the night went by with no thoughts of the odd things that had happened that day, just as he'd hoped it would. Most of his thoughts were actually occupied by the cute tour guide who had caught his eye the minute he got his job. Amy was tall, tan, with long blonde hair, and bright blue eyes - the girl belonged in a magazine, not showing tourists the mountains. But he couldn't believe his luck at getting to work with such a knockout. His heart soared every time she looked his way. Midnight fell, allowing a new day to begin and finding Tyler feeling just tired enough to walk to his bedroom. Pulling off his clothes and cracking the window to allow both the cool winter air and the sounds of the world slipping into sleep to flow into his room, he climbed into his bed and relaxed as the day's worries fell away, Amy on his mind as he felt sleep taking over.

***

Peace didn't follow him in his sleep, however. He was hounded through the night by images unlike any he'd ever experienced. The dream found him running through a large crowd of people, none of whom had a face, but all of whom were talking as loud as humanly possible. Panic set in quickly as he raced through the endless herd of faceless individuals, shoving them aside as he ran, looking for … what? He had no idea. Whatever it was, he was certain he was running out of time to find it. He stopped dead in his tracks as the crowd in front of him parted on their own without him having to push them aside anymore. The masses pulled back into themselves, out of his line of sight, revealing something that made his blood freeze in his veins.

A large creature stood in front of him, black as night and every bit of eight feet tall. Jagged fangs jutted from its mouth as it snarled, glowing red eyes meeting Tyler's in an instant. His breath hitched in his chest as his body chilled over. He had no idea what to do. The first thing he'd seen in this crowd that had any sort of features at all was now glaring at him with a look of hatred unmatched by anything he'd ever witnessed. Saliva dripped from the open jaws of the beast, running down its chest, matting up and darkening the hair there. As he watched, unable to turn away, the thing licked its lips and raised its arms. He watched as what looked like a bastardized cross between human hands and animal paws clenched tightly, blood oozing from the skin as two-inch claws ripped through flesh to get at the muscle and veins below.

He studied the creature from head to toe, marveling over how it balanced on legs that he could barely distinguish from a dog's. Large muscles bulged in the thighs, leading down to a thin, bowed tibia, with the firm, stocky tarsus taking all its weight. As he watched, the creature tensed, every muscle in its body seeming to double in size as it crouched, looking ready to pounce. As it lowered itself to the ground, Tyler saw a thick tail swish back and forth before pointing down towards the ground, revealing another person standing behind the creature. This man, thin and frail, looking terrified, was the only human in the crowd that had features. The man's eyes met his and instantly Tyler recognized the deep blue gaze of his father. Shrunken and withered, he couldn't believe this specimen was the man he once thought looked so strong and firm. He remembered his father's tall, wiry frame, how he always seemed to tower over him, and this cowering figure was nothing like the father he'd grown up with.

"Tyler," his father said, his voice small and distorted, as if being heard from a long distance. "Tyler, stay in the car."

"What," he said, not understanding what his father meant. He wasn't in a car. He was standing in a crowd of people, suddenly maddeningly aware of how exposed he was.

"Don't get out. Stay in the car."

His father's mouth continued to move, but his voice was drowned out as the beast in front of him began to emit a growl that shook Tyler's very lungs. It dropped to all fours and began creeping forward, growling louder as it did, the distance between the two of them growing smaller by the second. Tyler heard the voice of his father one last time as the thing took a breath and stood again, sparing him from seeing the cowering man's face as his voice was carried to him from behind the towering monster.

"Tyler," the voice said pleadingly. "Tyler, nooooo," the voice was drowned out as the hellish creature that now stood little more than an arm's length from Tyler howled a deathly, mournful howl. The sound was so loud and shocking that it made Tyler jerk himself awake.

Sitting up in bed, he tried hard to catch his breath and rid his mind of the sound of howling. He realized just as the sound began to taper off that it was coming from outside of his window, rather than in his head.

***

Tyler spent the rest of the night staring at his second-floor window, certain he would see the face of the monster from his dream staring in at him if he so much as blinked. He trembled, a cold sweat soaking through his bed clothes as he remembered the dream, seeing it play out over and over again, the look of fear on his father's face burned into his brain. Why would he have such a strange dream? More so, why would he have a dream about his father on the same day that he heard the man's voice come through on his car radio?

But that must be it, he thought. He'd had the dream because of what he'd heard on the radio. It must be. That's why the version of his father in the dream had said almost the exact same thing. That had to be it. But if that was the case, why had he envisioned his father so different than the man he remembered? It must be psychological, the academic in him said. He must internally view his father as small and weak, whether he admitted it or not. But what about that monster, that howl? He'd lived here for almost a year and he had never heard anything like that. He knew there were coyotes in the mountains, had even witnessed a few of them during the spring and summer, but somehow that didn't seem right. Would the small coyotes in this area really make a sound that loud and horrible? Plus, he realized, he had no idea just how much of the sound from his dream had come from this outside source and how much his own brain had created in response to the stimulus.

His head began to hurt from a mix of overthinking and a lack of sleep as the sun's first rays pierced the air, slipping in his partially open window, warming his face. He felt a sense of comfort as the day grew lighter, knowing somehow that whatever threats the night posed were not present in the day. He closed his eyes for a moment, feeling his body tense again as he saw the frightened face of his father. His stomach clenched, causing him to double over, suddenly very nauseated. Why was he seeing his father like this? Could all of this really just be because he had some strange radio interference yesterday? He had no idea if that could be the cause of his issues, but he knew that he would not be able to get the thoughts out of his head if he didn't at least try to contact his father.

***

Tyler breathed deeply of the steam-filled air, his lungs relishing the moist heat. He scrubbed his body all over, trying to wash the trauma of the night away with the remnants of his sweat. He went over his decision again as he showered, unsure if he'd made the right choice. He knew his father was a busy man, so busy that he rarely had time to see his family, and as a consequence they hadn't spoken in years. He wasn't even certain if the number he had would still be valid, but knew if he didn't try there would be no rest for his weary mind. Finishing his shower, he walked through his small house and started a fresh pot of coffee, hating that he needed it. As a rule, he tried to limit his intake of caffeine to soda, sweet tea, and his rare trips to the local chain specializing in over-priced specialty espressos after seeing his grandparents' addiction to the drug, but he had a feeling that today he would need an extra dose if he wanted to be fully functional.

As the smell of fresh Colombian blend filled his kitchen he sat down and looked through his phone for the last number he had for his father. He hadn't spoken to the man in over three years and wasn't even sure if his father would be willing to say anything to him. He knew his mother had told him that Tyler had relocated, and last he heard the old man wasn't very happy about it. He dialed the number and put the phone to his ear, suddenly painfully aware of the oppressive silence filling his house. The phone rang and rang, the tiny sound on the other end coming ten times before he stopped counting. He heard his father's voice say hello and almost responded before it went on to say that he was sorry he couldn't answer and would you please leave a message.

"Hey Dad," he said, hating talking to a machine. "It's Tyler. I know we haven't spoken in a while. I hope you're doing good. I just wanted to call and talk a bit. I've had a weird couple of days and I just...well, just give me a call back, OK?"

He recited the number from memory in case his father had forgotten it and hung up the phone, feeling even worse than he had before he made the call. What had prevented his father from answering the phone? He looked at the clock on his phone and saw it was just after 9. It must be a meeting. Without really thinking about it he decided to call his mother. She answered on the third ring in a frenzy.

"Tyler, what's wrong?"

"Hey Mom, nothing I hope. Why?"

"Well, you haven't called me at 9 a.m. in almost 5 years unless there was a problem."

"Well, it might be nothing, but I had a strange dream and tried to call Dad."

"You had a dream you called your father?"

"No. I had a really strange dream that involved Dad, so I just tried to call him to check on him. He didn't answer."

"Oh. Well, did you leave a message?"

"Yeah. Have you talked to him lately?"

"Uh…," she began, seeming unusually defensive. "No. Not really."

"Not really? Yes, or no, Mom. It was a pretty simple question."

"It's been a few months since I've had an actual conversation with him, but he sent me a strange text a couple of days ago."

"What did it say?"

"Not much, really. He just asked if you were safe."

"Why is that strange?"

"It was just out of the blue. Like I told you before, he seemed to be a bit upset to find out that you had moved to the Smokies, but I don't think he's asked me that question since you turned 15."

"Oh. Did he seem OK?"

"I don't know, Tyler," she said, obviously uncomfortable and, he thought, keeping some part of this interaction to herself. "It was just a text. I told him you were fine and that was it."

"All right," he said, knowing that once she closed up there was no changing her mind.

"Do you want to tell me about your dream?"

"It was just strange," he said, slightly touched that she was actually trying to be a mother for the first time in a long time. "I was in a crowd of people with no faces, and then I saw this monster. Dad was behind it. It howled at me and creeped me out. I think I had the dream because there was a coyote outside howling. I heard it when I woke up."

"You had your windows closed, right? It couldn't get in could it?"

"Well no, but I'm on the second floor, so it couldn't have anyway."

"Keep your windows closed, Tyler. You can't be too careful with things like this."

"Mom, I'm on the second floor."

"I don't care, Tyler," she said frantically. "You live down there in that God forsaken place and anything could happen. You could be murdered by...anything. And I'd never know."

"Mom, what's going on?"

"Nothing," she said, a little too fast. "I'm just worried about my only son, honey. You can't just live down there and let anything happen to you. There are people that care about you"

"I know. I'm not just letting anything happen to me. I'm living."

"I know. I know. I just worry about you. I don't want to lose you."

"You aren't. Are you sure you're OK?"

"I'm fine," she said in a voice that dared him to contradict her.

"Alright. You know you can call me if you ever need anything, right?"

"Of course. Thank you, though. It means a lot that you would say it."

"No problem. I love you, Mom."

"I love you, too, Tyler," she said, seeming surprised he even said it.

"I hate to go, but I need to get ready for work."

"Go ahead, honey. And don't hold stock in dreams, OK? Don't let these things get to you."

"Sure thing, Mom."

His mind was racing as he hung up the phone. His mother was obviously keeping something to herself. What it was and why, he had no idea. He poured himself a cup of coffee, cutting the bitter darkness with a hefty amount of liquid creamer and grabbed a pack of foil wrapped pastries to eat while he pulled on his clothes.

As he was getting dressed the thought of his father wouldn't leave him. There must be some other way to get in touch with him. But how? He wasn't in touch with anyone from his father's side of the family. The story he'd always heard was that his grandmother disapproved of the marriage and never forgave it. Meaning she wanted nothing to do with Tyler's mother and, in consequence, Tyler himself. He suspected this could have something to do with the fact that Tyler's parents had become serious shortly after the death of Tyler's grandfather, while his parents were both teenagers. With no grandfather, and a grandmother who pretended he didn't exist, Tyler didn't have any real connection to the Randolphs, so family was out of the question. If only he had managed to meet his father's boss, or even get the name of the company he worked for, but that never came up in conversation, which he didn't actually find odd until just now.

As he pondered this it hit him. Brad. His father's best friend. He'd practically seen Brad more than he had his own father some years during his childhood. Of course Brad would be able to explain what was going on. In any case, it couldn't hurt. He dialed the number quickly and waited impatiently until the man answered.

"Hello," came the familiar rasp that he hadn't heard in years.

"Brad," he asked, hoping he still had the same number.

"Yeah, who's this?"

"It's Tyler Randolph."

"Little Ty Randolph?! You're not serious!"

"Sure am."

"What in the world are you up to?"

"Not a whole lot. How are you these days?"

"I'm great, actually. Your mom tells me you're living in the mountains now."

"Yes sir. I've fallen in love with them."

"That's great. If I recall Jack had a particular affinity for the mountains, too."

"Really? That's pretty cool. Dad is actually one of the reasons I called."

"Oh," he said, as if he had already figured that out. "How can I be of assistance, bud?"

"Well, I was trying to get in touch with him, but his phone just went to voicemail. I've had-," he began, trying to decide if he should tell Brad everything. "I've had a strange couple of days. He's been on my mind."

"Well, buddy, I don't much know how I can help you. His number is the same, of course."

"Well, I know. I was actually wondering if you'd spoken to him lately. Maybe he'd told you if he had a meeting this morning, or at least that he was OK."

"I'm sorry Tyler, I haven't spoken to your dad in a couple of weeks. Last I heard from him he was doing fine, though. He said he'd been dealing with some difficult things, but that's to be expected. "

"What sort of things?"

"I'm not really sure. He mentioned something about family illness or something. He was in a bit of a hurry and wasn't making much sense."

"And that's the last time you heard from him?"

"Yep. I'm sorry, bud, is everything OK?"

"Well, I don't know. I had a weird experience yesterday and a strange dream last night and it's made me really feel like I need to talk to him. I'm afraid something might be wrong," he said, not realizing just how worried he was about this until the words fell from his mouth.

"You had a dream?"

"I know it sounds dumb, but it was really weird. My dad was in it, trying to protect me from something. He didn't look anything like I remember him, though. I could tell it was him, but he looked shriveled, weak."

"Well, buddy, your dad's never been a big guy. I remember the day that happened with my dad, though. I used to think he was huge and tough and then one day I looked at him and he was just a normal guy. It can definitely throw you off."

"I understand that, but I didn't see him in person, I just dreamed him. I think that's what strange. He didn't look like I remember him and it makes me worried. Are you sure he didn't say anything else?"

"I'm sorry, Tyler, that's all I know."

"OK. Thanks, Brad. If you hear from him can you let me know? And tell him to call me?"

"Absolutely, buddy. It's good to hear from you. I hope you get everything figured out."

"Thanks, me too. Take care, Brad."

Silence filled his house again after he hung the phone up. What sort of family illness could his father have been talking about? Or was Brad mistaken about that. Maybe his father had been sick. Could it be that his father had a serious illness and he was in a hospital somewhere? Maybe that's what his mother was trying to hide. He stopped himself before his mind went farther, knowing what his next "what if" was going to be. It wasn't possible, though. His father was fine. Whatever was going on here had nothing to do with his father's health. Why was he so worried to begin with? He'd just had a strange dream and heard a voice on the radio. That's it. He laughed at himself as the absurdity of his actions sank in. He was seriously sitting here scared to death that his father was in danger because of a silly dream? He must be losing it.

He put the thoughts of the last 18 hours out of his mind as best he could and finished his makeshift breakfast, knowing he'd be ravenous in a matter of hours. Making sure the coffee pot was off, he closed the door and left for work, turning up the radio as a particularly good song came. As he got closer to work he couldn't help but think of Amy again, the thought of her face working perfectly to drown out the leftover sense of worry in his mind.

***

Tyler made it to work a few minutes early and managed to fit in a little flirting with Amy before the day really started. As he waited for his own group to fill up so he could take them on the tour of the woods and cave system, he flipped through his phone, letting the day's latest social media drama pull him out of the world for a moment. Without thinking about it, he checked the weather forecast and was glad to see that there was little chance of rain until the end of the week and no snow for the foreseeable future.

"Excuse me, sir," someone in front of him said, pulling him back into the present. "Will we be leaving soon?"

"Let me see," he said, counting heads and coming up at 9. "I usually prefer to wait until we have a full group, but I think we can make this work. So sure! I'm sorry to have kept y'all waiting. My name is Tyler, and I'll be your guide for today," he said, starting his routine with an extra bit of vernacular and Southern charm directed at the lady who had suddenly regained her composure when she caught his smile coming her way.

The tour lasted around 45 minutes, with a nice hike through the woods, past a small cabin built beside the creek that ran from the cave system above. He stopped and opened the door of the old place to let the group see the inside, giving them time to step inside and glance around the large, bare room and ask any questions they desired. After a few moments he redirected their attention to the stream and explained that its source was a freshwater spring deep in the heart of the cave system. It had been the object of much study over the last 20 or so years as the tourism industry grew and local biologists caught what fish and animals they could flowing out in the clear, cool waters.

After this explanation, he took his group up to the entrance of the cave, where he gave everyone the opportunity to enter or wait, warning them that the floor was moist, steep and led into a cool antechamber that maintained a steady 58 degrees year-round. Everyone was eager to enter the cave and see what sort of strange rock formations they could see, many of them voicing an interest in seeing some form of darkness-loving creature in its natural habitat. As he went through the cavern he felt, like usual, that he was in an amazing place that time had created unintentionally. He loved the cave system and had actually explored far beyond the boundaries he was allowed to go with a group, finding that the miles and miles of caves held more beauty than he could have ever expected. Despite his love for the cavern, he couldn't keep himself from constantly checking his phone, hoping beyond hope that his father would be calling him back any time.

When his first tour was over and he'd gotten more than one suggestive glance from the mother who had first spoken to him, he said goodbye to them and thanked them for their interest in what he now called "our beautiful mountains". This was a phrase he loved to use and, since his first time using it around other guides, had become almost part of the script for them as well.

Sitting down on an old portion of stone wall by the side of the waiting area, he felt the cool breeze blow across his face, hearing the sounds of the forest around him slowly die down as something rustled through the underbrush. The hair on the back of his neck stood up as a twig snapped behind him, causing him to turn around and peer into the darkness. Whatever was there ceased its movements, no more noise coming from the brush before him. He took a step closer to the wall, knowing the decision may not be a wise one if the creature in the woods proved to be a hungry bear that had ventured out in the unusually warm weather to search for a nice mid-winter snack. Silence hung heavily on the air as the sounds of the current tour group followed the beaten path behind their guide, leaving him alone for the moment. His mind ran rampant with images of the monster he'd dreamed about, hearing his father's pleading tone that he just stay in the car. He leaned forward a bit more, fancying that he could almost make out a shadow in the underbrush.

As he stared into the darkness a sudden sound made him jump nearly out of his skin. A squirrel in a nearby tree, clearly feeling threatened by him, began to bark loudly, breaking the silence. This sound was followed by a sudden thrashing in the woods that made Tyler back away quickly, tripping over the uneven pathway behind him. He froze on the ground, certain he was about to be face to face with the monster from his dream, covering his face when a deer burst through the underbrush. The dainty, frightened animal leaped over the wall, landing a foot from Tyler's prone figure, bounding away when it realized it had gotten so close to another living being. Tyler turned his head to watch the deer run up the path and back into the woods as it neared the tour group.

He lay on the ground for a moment, realizing that his heart was beating away at the inside of his rib cage like a prisoner desperately wanting freedom. He began laughing as he realized he'd almost had a heart attack because of a little deer. He laid back completely, putting his hand in a pile of leaves as the laughter rolled and roared out of him while the squirrel above continued in its attempts to annoy him into leaving.

"What's so funny, City Slicker," came a voice from behind him.

He sat up quickly, turning to see the cute guide, Amy, standing there, regarding him with a grin that made her whole face light up.

"Oh not much, beautiful. Just had my life threatened by a squirrel and a deer."

"Wow, you really must not have had many animals back home if those two scare you. Down here we eat those with biscuits and don't think twice."

"Is that so," he asked playfully as he stood and dusted himself off. "That might be something worth trying."

"It's something everyone should try at least once," she said, taking a step closer to him as she did. "I was actually thinking about fixing some on Sunday if you're interested."

"You just have deer and squirrel laying around to cook at any time?"

"Deer. I never really liked squirrel."

"Well, I'll try anything once."

"Sunday at my place?"

"If you can stand the company of a Yankee in your humble abode, my sweet Southern Belle," he said, playfully throwing out the nickname he knew made her laugh.

"I think I can handle one cute one, at least," she said, blushing as she made the comment.

"Well, let me know when you find one cute enough to tolerate," he said, stepping over until he was standing right in front of her. "I'd like to shake his hand for winning such a prize."

"Well," she said, moving even closer, "I think I might have found one."

He leaned in, wanting nothing more than to kiss the girl who'd had his attention for months, terrified that she would change her mind. His lips touched hers lightly, before she reacted, pushing into him firmly as he pulled her closer. He had no idea how long they remained like that, but he knew that he didn't want it to end. Once they finally separated neither knew who had initiated it, but both knew it was the best kiss they'd ever experienced.

"So, Sunday," he said, holding her by the waist, feeling like he'd just changed the world.

"Sunday," she said, looking into his eyes, a look of satisfaction that he would never forget on her face.

"Your place?"

"Unless you'd rather go somewhere else. I'm only about five minutes from here. You're welcome to follow me tonight if you'd like to. Just so you can see where it is, of course," she said, unable to hide her blush as she suggested it.

"I'd love to," he replied, feeling like his life had just improved once again. Leaning in, he stole one more kiss before they heard the sound of someone walking back down the trail towards them, signaling the end of the last tour before lunch break.

The pair stepped back, holding hands as they walked to the edge of the path to let the group pass by. Kayla, the other female tour guide with the company walked by last, having made sure the entire group left the system safely. She glanced at the pair, looking slightly confused as they both blushed, but unable to contain her excitement when she saw they were holding hands. She quickly said goodbye to her group at the end of the trail and ran back to them practically jumping up and down.

"You guys," she said in a loud, excited whisper. "Oh my gosh, tell me all about it. What happened?"

They looked at each other and smiled, Tyler nodding to Amy to tell her to take it away.

"We were talking and we just kind of... kissed," she said shyly.

"It's really about time," Kayla said seriously. "You two have been making eyes at each other since Tyler first walked in. If it didn't happen soon I was going to push you in that cabin and lock you in until you figured it out!"

They laughed as she congratulated them and walked down to the small kitchen to grab something for lunch, knowing the next tour group would be lining up in just under an hour. Tyler and Amy decided they would go grab something and walk back up to the cabin, wanting to see how Kayla's idea would work after all. They toted a couple of sandwiches and some fruit up to the front porch of the cabin, sitting with their legs swinging over the edge, the food behind them. As they ate they talked about their lives, getting to know each other a little better as the hour went on. Tyler felt himself growing more and more connected with Amy as she told him about herself. She liked many of the same things as he did, and had actually moved here on her own just a year before he did. He was a few months older than her, a fact that she seemed to enjoy, saying in the past she'd only dated guys who were a little younger than her.

Tyler felt himself straying away from the subject of his parents while Amy discussed her own, hoping that she didn't pick up on the strange look that crossed his face when she asked what his father did. The hour passed quickly, both of them realizing at the same time that Kayla was bringing a group that looked to contain about 20 people up the hill towards them. They hopped off the porch, leaving the remains of their lunch beside the cabin to be picked up later and rushed down to the group.

"Hey, Kayla," Tyler said quickly. "Do you want me to split the group with you?"

"I think I've got this one. You kids go on," she said, gesturing to the fact that most of the people in her large group were older. Kayla had worked at the Douglas Cabin and Cave System for over ten years and had had her share of large groups. She winked at them again as they walked away, brushing hands before grasping them and walking together.

"Do you think she'll be OK with a group that big," Amy asked, knowing it might be a little hard if they were younger people.

"Oh yeah, she'll be fine. I saw her make one group of teenagers go completely silent with just a look. She's got this."

They went to the foot of the path and stood side by side as more people filed in, separating into the proper lines. Amy's group filled first and she took them up the hill, smiling at Tyler as she asked them to follow her.

The rest of the day seemed to crawl by in the moment, but as the last group left, Tyler realized he had no idea where the time had gone. He and Amy met up with Kayla in what served as a kitchen and break room of their small tourist center as they did at the end of every day.

"So, do you guys have any plans," she asked with a smile.

"Actually," Amy spoke up. "Tyler is following me to my place so he knows where I live. I'm cooking the poor boy dinner on Sunday."

"Uh-Oh," Kayla laughed. "You must be a glutton for punishment, Tyler."

The three laughed as Amy explained that Tyler had never had venison and she felt it was her responsibility to fix that mistake.

"I understand completely. Well, don't let me hold you all up. I'll lock up here if you want to go on."

"Are you sure," Tyler said. "We don't want to put you out any."

"Please. You kids have a good night. You both deserve it. I'll see you tomorrow."

They said goodnight to her and walked to their cars, discussing the plan for the short trip.

"Just follow me out and we'll go to my place," Amy said shyly. "If that's still OK."

"It sounds great to me," he said boldly.

They smiled at each other again and got into their cars, Tyler not able to believe his luck. The trip really didn't take more than five minutes. He pulled into the driveway behind Amy, seeing a house that was a little larger than his own. Her brick home was complete with a birdbath in the front yard and a quaint garden of flowers along the side of her porch. Twin rocking chairs decorated one side of the porch while an old fashioned bench swing filled the other. He got out as Amy did, smiling as she looked back at him nervously.

"This might sound silly," he started, suddenly afraid he'd misunderstood. "But you didn't intend for me to follow you here and leave right away, did you?"

"I hadn't actually thought this far," she said, laughing, her tension seeming to melt as he walked up to her. "But I'm glad you didn't leave."

"So am I," he said as she took his hand and walked him up to her front door.

Amy's house instantly impressed him. The scent of apples and wildflowers seemed to fill the air just enough to be pleasantly noticed. She gave him the tour of the house, beginning with the living room, which was adorned with pictures from a number of places he'd fallen in love with since his move to the mountains. He mentioned this as she paused over a few of them, gaining a huge smile from her as she learned that he knew and loved each one as much as she did. The kitchen, done in a modest beige with a slight farmhouse theme, was clean and well stocked he noticed as she showed him nearly everything she could imagine. She skimmed over the minor details of the laundry room, downstairs bathroom and basement, telling him those were fairly standard and he was welcome to see them any time.

He could tell she was nervous as she walked him upstairs. The first stop on this leg of the tour was the guest room, which she had furnished with a television and more photos of the region, the room painted a solid blue which reflected lightly off the highly polished hardwood floors. The upstairs bathroom was given the same treatment as the downstairs one, another open invitation given as they walked toward the only other door on the second floor. She paused outside the door, turning and looking him in the eyes for the first time since entering the house.

"I'm really nervous."

"Why?"

"I've never had a guy in my house before. Especially not in my bedroom."

"I understand. We can save this part for another time, if you're uncomfortable. I'm not pushing you to do anything you don't want. I'm just as nervous as you are."

"It's not that. I'm not uncomfortable. I guess it's just that you seem different. I've never known anyone quite like you."

"I hope that's a compliment, because I think the same, and it's certainly good on my end."

"I think it's great. I feel really at ease with you. I guess that's why I seem tense, if that makes sense."

"Completely. You're not nervous because it feels natural, but the fact that your guard seems down is making you overcompensate?"

"Yes. Exactly. You too?"

"Oh yeah."

She smiled wider than ever and stepped backward into her bedroom, leading him by the hand into the room that no one but her mother had ever entered. Amy's bedroom was adorned with her personal artwork, all hand-painted and drawn in the small office that was off to the side of her room. Paintings of landscapes, sweeping rivers, sunsets, and more were displayed on the walls of the bedroom and the office.

"Are these your work," he asked, impressed.

"Yes. What do you think?"

"I think they're amazing," he said, smiling at her as she blushed again.

"Thank you. Painting has always been a passion of mine."

"Well, you're very good at it."

She stepped back to the bed, sitting on the edge and inviting him to join her. They looked at each other for a moment before he broke the silence.

"Um, Amy?"

"Yes?"

"You're very beautiful. I can't believe I haven't told you sooner."

"Thank you," she said, leaning forward and kissing him lightly. He pressed back for just a moment, feeling her tension and not wanting her to think he was being pushy.

"Would you like to go out and grab some dinner?"

"Why, Mr. Randolph," she said, playing the offended damsel. "Are you asking me on a date?"

"Well, Ms. Turner, that was my intention," He said, with a hint of his own imitation of a Southern accent.

"I'd love to. Which, since you're here, we could cook here tonight and go out Sunday. Whichever you'd prefer."

"Lady's choice. I'm just lucky to be with you."

She blushed yet again before kissing him once more and pulling him to his feet. "Well, since the meat I was planning on cooking is frozen solid, I think I'll let you take me out on the town."

"Sounds perfect to me, beautiful," he said as he let her lead him back to the front door.

They rode to the city in Tyler's car, talking the whole way about anything and everything, becoming more and more comfortable with each other with each passing minute. Tyler took her to the restaurant she said she'd been dying to try and they parked in a public lot and walked in rather than ride the public transportation into the themed area. They held hands the entire way, laughing and talking in happiness. The rest of the night went by in a blur that neither would forget. After they finished their dinner they walked around and peeked in some of the shops and enjoyed a live band playing a bit of classic country music before walking back to Tyler's car.

"Is there anywhere else you'd like to go, Amy? The night is young."

"I don't think ten is too young," she laughed. "I've had an amazing time, but I can think of two things that would make my night even better. Hopefully you'll only laugh at one of them."

"Your wish is my command, madam."

"I would kill for some ice cream," she said laughing. "And then I would really love it if we could go sit on my porch for a bit."

"Both of those things sound amazing."

***

Tyler and Amy got back to her house by 11 and took up residence on her porch swing to enjoy the cooling night, their ice cream long gone. The view from her porch was breathtaking as the stars flashed and twinkled in their nest of deep blue, the moon providing just enough illumination to allow him to see Amy look at him in the dark. Her eyes twinkled, reflecting the light of the moon back into his. He kissed her deeply, feeling her melt as he wrapped his arms around her. She kissed him back, her tongue lightly playing around the edge of his mouth as he ran his hands through her hair. They kissed, lightly caressing each other without the slightest hesitation until a loud truck roared around the curve, breaking the peaceful sounds of the night and illuminating them with an almost blinding nonchalance. They pulled back, almost feeling as if they were teenagers who'd just been caught by their parents.

"I've had a really great time tonight, Amy."

"So have I. I don't think I've ever had a date this great."

"I know I haven't," he said, tucking her hair behind her ear as a breeze blew it across her face.

"Where do we go from here?"

"I guess that's really up to you. I have no expectations of anything, and believe me, I'm not going to disappear. Unless that's what you want."

"It isn't. Not at all. I am getting a little tired, though. Maybe we could call it a night?"

"As you wish, beautiful. I'll see you tomorrow?"

"You will. Drive safe, OK?"

"Of course," he said, standing and walking her to her door. "Would you mind if I stayed until I know you get inside safely?"

"I'd actually prefer it," she said, stretching up to give him one more lingering kiss before saying goodnight and unlocking her door.

***

Tyler's drive home was full of thoughts of Amy. He'd wanted to take her out since the day he saw her, and he could barely believe it had happened. The road unfolded in front of him as he made the half hour drive between her house and his, the familiar turns and curves not needing much thought as he drove through the darkness. How could he have been so lucky? What's more, how could she be single? Her shy nature could be an easy explanation for this question, but how could they be so natural together? He didn't hold much stock in fate, but felt the answer could be somewhere in that field, meaning it lay far outside of his jurisdiction. His thoughts were interrupted by a loud burst of static from the radio, the station resuming quickly as the interference passed, leaving him to his thoughts as his driveway came into view.

Once he got home he went straight to his bedroom, pulled off his clothes and dove into bed after cracking the window again, not thinking for a second of his mother's request. His mind was full of Amy again. He turned onto his side, sleep suddenly coming to him after his long day. He drifted off with a smile on his face. His happiness faded fast as he began dreaming.

He was running through the woods, his heart pounding in his chest. He knew, somehow, that something was after him, and he also knew that he wasn't alone. His breath was ragged and hot in his throat, burning with each inhalation. Branches slapped and scratched his face, making his eyes water. As he ran on he heard large, pounding footsteps behind him, keeping pace with him as if trying to wear him down.

Looking to his right he saw a thin, hunched shadow, pale skin gleaming in the minimal light. As he watched the figure running with him, they entered a moonlit clearing, illuminating the fearful, dirt and blood streaked face of his father. The man looked at him as they ran, his eyes seeming to convey the urgency that they needed to keep going. He glanced ahead and saw an open clearing that seemed to go on forever and decided he had to try to get a glimpse of what was chasing them. He turned his head, glancing behind them once and almost tripping over a root that sprung up from nowhere.

"Tyler, don't, "his father warned urgently. "Don't look back. Never look back!"

"Why?"

His father didn't answer, but a strange look crossed his features for an instant. His countenance twisted and became a distorted mask of anger and frustration. Tyler stumbled again, his foot landing in a hole that collapsed from ground that had just been solid. It felt like he went down in slow motion, seeing everything around him go by, his father's eyes growing wider than ever as he realized Tyler was falling. Halfway down he heard more than felt the snap of his leg breaking as his body pushed the top half of his leg forward while he was buried to the shin in the unseen hole.

"Tyler," His father exclaimed, his voice mixing with a roar of triumph from behind them.

The man who had always seemed so large now moved to stand between him and their oncoming attacker. Growls filled the air as the sound of slapping paws slowed a bit. Tyler pulled himself from the hole, twisting his body as agony filled his leg. He knew that, whatever was coming, he had to be there to see it. The footsteps stopped, sounding as if they were right in front of his father, but Tyler could see nothing. Moonlight still illuminated the entire clearing, but there was only grass in front of his father.

He heard the sound of growls rise slowly, his father's voice just under the sound, making pitiful whimpers, saying "no" repeatedly as the growls rose. Soon the snarling overpowered his father's voice until only the ravenous and angry sounds of the creature could be heard. He saw his father's body bend and twist, the muscles under his now very tight shirt bulging and rippling with every movement. He pulled himself away from the hunched figure before him as a whimper of pain that almost sounded like his name poured into the night. He didn't know what was going on, but he knew there was something very wrong with his father. He had to try and help him.

"Dad? What's wrong?"

His father stiffened, his head turning slightly, as if listening closer for Tyler to speak again. The growls lowered until they were little more than a rumble that he could feel throughout his entire body. He slid back a little more, trying not to cry out when his broken, twisted leg caught on yet another root. His body slid over dead leaves and dry grass, the sound like a rasp of anger that seemed to echo in the open space. The figure in front of him hunched a little and began to turn, making his heart pound even harder. As much as he wanted to see his father and know what was wrong, he knew he didn't want him to turn around.

The sight was worse than anything Tyler could have imagined. His father's face was drawn back in a pitiful mix of pain and anger, glowing red eyes set deep in his deformed face. His nose seemed to have flattened against his face and his mouth protruded slightly, jagged fangs jutting from between his lips. Claws sprouted from the tips of his twisted fingers and his back bent more as his eyes met Tyler's. As Tyler watched thick, coarse black hair seemed to ooze from his father's pores, covering every inch of exposed skin. The thing in front of him ripped the shirt off its back with ease, dropping the shredded cloth to the ground. A tearing sound filled the night as the moonlight shone brighter than ever on the creature now stalking him as he began to tremble. Looking down he saw large, dog-like paws had torn apart the shoes his father had been wearing, the source of the ripping sound now obvious.

"Dad," he said, terrified. "What's happening to you? Is this even you? What's going on?"

The thing in front of him dropped to all fours and began to snarl, thick white foam dripping from its jaws as they elongated from the face that used to belong to his father, bringing the flattened nose with them to create a long, fang-filled snout. The jowls of the creature tightened, the thick black hair quickly covering the little exposed skin that remained. He watched as the creature's eyes slid farther apart and its ears elongated, erasing most of the resemblance this thing had to his father. It snapped at the air in front of its face once as the realization hit Tyler hard. His father was some kind of monster. He tried to stand, the broken ends of his tibia rubbing each other before sliding apart and making his leg collapse under him as he cried out in pain. The thing in front of him took a menacing step towards him but got hung up in the pants it still wore, causing it to fall on its face.

Anger filled its face as it howled in offended rage. It curled up and began to tear at the pant legs in an attempt to free itself from this unwelcome hindrance. Tyler, his pain greater than anything he'd ever felt, took the opportunity to try once again to escape. He stood, bracing his weight on his good leg and began to hop as fast as he could as he heard the sounds of ripping cloth and growls growing slightly fainter behind him. The edge of the woods now loomed close, looking just as safe as it did intimidating. He made it into the tree line before stopping to look behind him. The creature was just where he'd left it, fighting harder than ever with the pants that now looked as though they'd been put through a garbage disposal. It looked up, saw that he was gone and exploded in a rage that made Tyler quake in his temporary haven. Gaining some composure, or just drawing from his father's muscle memory, it reached for the waistband of the pants, ripping the buttons and zipper apart, allowing it to wiggle and kick its way out of the last thing that made it recognizable as a human.

It looked around the clearing for a moment, trying to decide where it should go to find its prey again. Tyler backed slowly into the woods, trying to figure out the safest way for him to get away. He backed into the trunk of a large oak tree as the beast in the moonlight lowered its snout to the ground and began sniffing the spot where he'd fallen. Getting the scent, it jerked its head upward, seeming to look Tyler right in the face before howling loudly into the night sky. Tyler knew he had to act quickly. He turned and found the lowest branch he could grab and began pulling himself up into the tree as fast as he could, using his good leg whenever he had the chance, trying to be as silent as possible. He was about ten feet off the ground when he heard the pounding of the beast running towards the woods, making him climb that much faster. He reached a thick, hardy branch he knew would hold his weight and would hopefully mask him from anything looking up from below. Turning his body so that his feet were braced against the tree trunk and his face was pointed down through the cover of thinner twigs and limbs, he lay completely still, having to force himself to stop trembling.

The thing entered the woods below him in a frenzy, tearing at the underbrush as if it thought every bush, every weed were Tyler himself. He watched as the sleek creature balanced itself on its large paws, bushy tail swishing back and forth in the air as it turned in every direction looking for him. It finally dawned on him what the thing looked like. He'd only seen one in person once when he'd gone to a zoo as a child, but the more he watched it the more he was certain that this thing somehow resembled a wolf. It was much bigger than any wolf he'd ever heard of, but the way it moved, the way it hunted and howled all made him think of the ones he'd seen in the zoo. He remembered how they'd made his father uneasy, eventually causing him to walk away on his own after his requests to Tyler's mother to walk on had fallen on deaf ears.

The wolf creature pushed through the underbrush all around the edge of the forest where it had tracked him, peering into the darkness as if it expected to see him watching it from a distance. It lowered its snout to the ground again, following the path he'd walked, coming back to the spot it had started at twice. It finally walked over to an area of the brush it hadn't yet inspected, instantly catching his scent and tracking it right to the tree trunk Tyler had climbed. It snarled loudly, looking up the trunk. Tyler didn't know how, but he was positive that it somehow picked him out of the branches and looked right into his eyes, the hatred it felt filling his own mind as it did.

At least wolves can't climb trees, he thought to himself, already knowing that his only option for survival was going to be laying still on his branch until the wolf grew tired or bored and went on to find other prey. He watched, feeling mild relief that he had climbed so high, as the creature seemed to weigh its options before rearing back and balancing on its hind legs, instantly making it feel so much closer to him despite the fact he was easily 40 feet from the ground.

"It can't climb," he told himself again. "I'm fine."

As this thought crossed his mind the wolf reached toward the trunk with its hand-like paws, grasping a branch in its fingers with ease before readjusting so it could pull itself off the ground a bit before lowering back down and trying again in a different position.

"Oh God," he thought, feeling panic flood through him again as adrenaline was dumped into his blood. "It's trying to learn to climb. What if it does? What do I do? What do I do?"

The wolf got a few feet off the ground before its back paws pedaled the air and caused it to lose its grip, falling back to the ground with an annoyed growl. It looked back up the tree towards Tyler before looking around itself again, giving him a sense of hope.

"Maybe it's going to leave," he hoped. "Or maybe it doesn't even know for sure that I'm up here. It hasn't seen me yet. As long as I don't move I should be ok."

The wolf stood tall again and leaped toward the trunk, wrapping its front paws around two branches and pulling itself up onto a third, digging its back paws into the bark for support when it started to slip. Fear filled Tyler again and more adrenaline flooded his brain, making him feel he needed to move. The wolf lifted its snout and sniffed the air, seeming to catch the change in Tyler's condition, making it climb with more urgency. It was now nearly ten feet off the ground, resting on a branch that was already bending in an effort to hold its weight. It looked around and found another branch to pull itself up with, now understanding how to use its back paws to help in its efforts.

It removed another ten feet from between them with little effort, pausing in its journey now that the branches were growing a bit thinner and more scattered. Tyler remained frozen to the spot, watching as the thing now leapt straight up, catching a thick branch that brought it 8 feet closer to Tyler. Four yards now separated the pair, Tyler realized. The wolf was probably over 7, maybe 8 feet tall on its hind legs, making it taller than half the distance he was counting on for survival. As he watched the wolf grasped another branch and pulled itself up, now finding a rhythm and killing the distance between itself and its prey with ease until it was just a few feet under him. Stretching its arms out, it dug its claws into the bark and looked up, now easily picking out Tyler's face from among the twigs. It roared triumphantly, looking straight into his eyes while adjusting itself to finish the climb. Tyler sat up now, knowing there was no reason to stay still. He reached to his right and pulled a fairly thick branch toward him, pushing against its base until it snapped in his hand, leaving him with only a makeshift spear to protect himself from the thing that was now balancing on the branch directly below his own.

He saw one hairy paw reach up and grasp the thick branch that had been his salvation, followed by another. The thing dug its claws into the wood as deep as it could and launched itself upwards from the branch it was on. It landed just feet from Tyler, looking right into its eyes as it did. It was clumsy in its jump, obviously eager to reach its prey and begin what he could only assume would be a satisfactory feast. The thing looked around it, checking to see if there was any better purchase so it could make its attack. Tyler saw his chance as the thing looked down at the branch from where it had just come. He lunged forward, jabbing his weapon at the wolf. The sharp wood entered the flesh of the creature's shoulder, throwing it off balance. It slid sideways down the branch, pulling the wood free of its body before catching itself, snarling and snapping its jaws in pain. It glared at Tyler, daring him to move as it crept around and braced itself on the branch once more. His breath was hitching in his chest. He watched the blood running down the wolf's shoulder, matting its fur down and coating the branch it was on. It growled deeply at him again as he braced himself, knowing now that he could hurt the thing that had somehow been impersonating his father.

He lunged forward again, jabbing at the wolf's chest with his spear, careful to use every inch of space he could to prevent from getting too close to the thing. The spear hit the wolf in the chest and slid sideways across its sternum. Tyler hadn't jabbed forward with enough force to kill it, but it definitely knew he wasn't going to be easy to dispose of now, he thought. The wolf howled in pain as its skin separated, more blood pouring out of it, now sounding like rain as it dripped onto the leaves below. It lunged forward and snapped at the branch in Tyler's hand. He reacted instinctively, swinging the branch around and catching the wolf in the jaw with the sharp edge and almost knocking it off of the thick branch. It backed up as far as it dared, its haunches now balancing precariously on the edge of the branch and growled at him deeply as it tried to find a way to beat this now formidable opponent.

Tyler waited, biding his time as the wolf bled more and more, hoping that the loss of blood would make it weak enough for him to get away. It grew impatient as he waited. It tensed its legs, preparing for action. Slowly it began to creep forward, its red eyes darting from Tyler's face to the branch he was now wielding like a shield. Tyler knew this may be his last chance for action and quickly formed a plan in his head. He let the wolf get about a foot closer to him before jabbing the branch at the thing's head. It reacted as he hoped, lifting itself up and snapping at the impending threat. He pulled the spear down at the last second and jammed it with all of his might into the chest of the wolf. It roared in pain, losing all of its former plan in the moment. It stood on its hind legs, digging its claws into the branch as best it could. Tyler tried to pull his weapon free, to no avail. He was picked up by the strength of his attacker, not thinking about letting go of the spear. The wolf wasn't thinking clearly either, significantly weakened by its climb up the tree and the loss of blood it had suffered. Its legs buckled once as it reached its full height. By some dark miracle it was able to catch itself and look Tyler in the eye just seconds before its feet slid out from under it, sliding right off the branch that had been thoroughly saturated by its blood.

Tyler relished in the sight of the thing falling from the branch for a split second before realizing that he was still holding onto his weapon and the wolf was taking him with it. He let go quickly, but it was too late. He crashed through the branches just behind the beast, catching himself on a branch that was thick enough to hold him up. He heard the thing crash into ground below him, heard the crack of bones as it met the Earth. Looking down he could see the wolf lying on the ground, its legs spread wide, the spear now jutting out of its back. Surely it must be dead, he thought. He lowered himself to the branch below him, keeping one eye on the wolf in case it still had some life in its broken body.

As he watched, the wolf began to twitch, its head looking around as its paws clenched into fists. It roared in pain as it tried to roll over. Tyler stopped where he was, balanced precariously above imminent danger on a branch that was dipping lower by the second. His broken leg throbbed fiercely, demanding he see a doctor and end the suffering. The wolf finally rolled over onto its side, the moonlight illuminating the inner edge of the woods enough for him to see that the red glow in its eyes had faded. Blood ran freely out of multiple wounds in the creature's body and pooled on the ground where it had landed. He watched as the thing began to twitch, every muscle in its body seeming to spasm wildly all at once. Its face shrank, the snout sliding back and flattening into a human mouth and jawline again, the hair falling out in patches all over its body as it began to sink into itself and deteriorate. The face stopped shrinking, but remained in a hideous mask, frozen in pain and anguish. Lips drawn back, covered in blood, there was no mistaking the now half-human figure on the ground below him. He saw the wolf recede inch by inch to reveal the broken and bleeding figure of his father.

A groan escaped his lips as he watched his father emerge from the mess of fur and blood, the broken limbs still unchanging. The figure below heard his groan and turned his head upwards, squinting his eyes in an effort to see into the darkness above.

"Tyler," his father wheezed as best he could, "is that you?"

The shock of hearing his father's voice come from the thing below him made him lose his grip, his legs collapsing under him, spilling him the last ten feet onto the ground. He landed in the pool of his father's blood, his broken leg grinding once again, the pain filling his brain and threatening to make him lose consciousness. He cried out softly, tears running down his blood and dirt streaked face as he looked over and saw his father in a twisted heap beside him. He had done this. But was it his fault?

36

Was this thing even his father? His mind raced with possibilities, trying to find an explanation that didn't mean he had just somehow tried to kill his own father. Or worse, that his father hadn't just tried to kill him.

"Dad," he whispered, looking into the eyes of the man lying in front of him, "is it really you? Oh God, I'm so sorry. Please forgive me. I don't know what's happening."

"It's me. It is. I know you don't. It isn't your fault. I'm fine. Tyler, I'm sorry. You saved me."

"How? I didn't save you, I just killed you."

"No. Son, thank you," his father said, fresh tears running down his cheeks. He reached out one of the furry paws that still refused to change back and caressed Tyler's face with it. "Promise me…"

"What, Dad? Anything. What?"

"Don't get out...car...stay…," he started, his life ending before he could get out the rest.

Tyler awoke as the sound of his father's last, long, raspy breath rang out in the dream. When he came to in his own dark room, he still heard the sound of breathing coming from somewhere. He had no idea what it was, but he was certain that it wasn't his.

***

Tyler sat up in bed, listening to the wheezing breath that filled the room. There was no way anyone could be in here, was there? No. He was certain of it. The first thing he noticed was that the door was still closed. As he moved, he was certain his leg would prevent him from making a getaway before he remembered it wasn't actually broken. He reached down quickly to be sure, finding that there was nothing wrong with either leg. He stood quickly, and walked towards his door. As he crossed the small room he heard a rustling from outside of his window and instantly realized that's where the breathing was coming from. He slowly crossed the room, terrified there would be a wolf standing below his window looking up at him.

Peering out into the darkness, he didn't see anything. Clouds had rolled in as he slept, making the already dark side of his house impossibly black. He grabbed a flashlight from his nightstand and went back, raising the window enough to stick the light out and turn it on. The cone of bright light gave him a view of the bare branches below the window, the noise of the light switching on making whatever was outside more alert. He heard the rustling again. Circling the light around once, he caught sight of a black shadow and nearly dropped it in shock. He moved it back around to where he thought he'd seen the shadow and heard the pounding of paws on the ground. A shadow ran through his light as he moved it, making him jump again as the sound of running continued. He moved the light around a few more times, trying to find whatever it was. He stopped moving the light to catch his breath and the shadow entered the small cone again, snapping at the light.

He nearly yelled in the night, certain it was the wolf from his dream come to take its revenge. He looked closely at the shadow nipping at the edges of his light and realized that it was much smaller than the wolf in his dream had been. It was also lighter in color, and was wagging its tail. He felt stupid as he realized it was just a dog, probably lost and afraid, who had chased his light in an attempt to play. He whistled heartily, laughing to himself as the dog looked up, tongue lolling out of its mouth and wagged its tail harder.

"Wait there, boy," he said. "I'm coming down."

He ran down the stairs and opened the back door, heart still pounding from an excess of adrenaline. He flipped the kitchen light on, stepped outside and whistled again, laughing this time as he heard the running dog approach. He stepped back into the doorway as he saw the shadow round the corner and closed the door behind the dog as it leapt up, covering his neck and face with saliva.

"Calm down," he said, laughing. "Down boy!"

Wherever the dog had come from, it had picked up at least a few commands. It sat promptly on the floor on the floor as he asked and looked to his hand as it wagged its tail.

"You're expecting a treat now, huh? Well wait right there. Stay," he said as he walked to the fridge and grabbed a slice of cheese.

He unwrapped the cheese and broke it into three pieces, tossing the first to the dog before moving. It caught the cheese in midair and swallowed it without even chewing. He walked over and fed it the other two pieces while checking its neck for a collar. The dog ate as if it hadn't seen food in weeks. He found no form of identification on the animal, but could tell it must have been well loved very recently. The dog had clearly been recently groomed and its manners were quite good. Someone must be missing this pooch a lot.

"Where do you come from, boy," he asked, as if expecting the dog to speak up. It licked his hand in response and sat back down, looking around the house. "Go ahead and explore a bit."

It was as if the dog had awaited permission, but now roamed the kitchen from wall to wall, nose to the floor sniffing and chuffing along as if in search of its next meal. The thought gave him cold chills, making his legs go weak under him. He dropped into one of the kitchen chairs, envisioning the nightmare again. As he did a new thought dawned on him. The creature he had just faced had been familiar to him. He had dreamed about it the night before as well. Two nights in a row he had been plagued by this monster in his sleep, and both nights it had something to do with his father. Something was very strange here, and Tyler thought it would be in his best interest to figure out what it was.

The rest of the night went by quickly. Tyler found some bread for the dog and fed it some more cheese, filling a water bowl three times before it had drank its fill. He let the dog follow him to his room where it curled up beside his bed and was asleep before he'd even laid down. He knew the dog was exhausted, but so was he, so this was one mystery he knew had to wait for another day.

***

He pulled into work early the next morning, beyond happy to see that Amy's car was already there. He opened the door and went into the office with a smile on his face, despite the bags under his eyes. Amy met him halfway through the kitchen, a fresh cup of coffee in her hand.

"Good morning, handsome," she said with a smile. "How was your night?"

"It was very different," he said, returning her smile. "I was going to text you when I got home, but I didn't want to disturb you."

"You wouldn't have. I thought of the same, actually. You look like you didn't get much sleep."

"Well, to be honest I didn't."

"Oh," she said with a wink.

He laughed a bit and planted a kiss on her cheek before sitting her down to explain the rest of his night. He toned the nightmare down quite a bit, just telling her he dreamed something was chasing him and that he woke up to hear something panting. When he told her about the dog her eyes grew huge. He finished up by telling her that he was going to put up some flyers and call around in the next few days, but that he needed to go buy some food and things after work that day.

"Can I come," she asked immediately. "I love dogs!"

"Of course. If you want you can follow me to my place and we'll ride to the store together afterwards."

"That sounds great!"

With their plans all set, Tyler joined her in a cup of coffee and they went through five tours through the day, the two of them taking the last one together, their boss noticing their sudden close behavior as well. Once the last group had left he asked them to join him in his office before they left.

"Can I ask what's going on between you two," he asked frankly.

"We're uh...Well, we're kind of dating," Tyler said, feeling it was his responsibility to speak up.

"When did this happen," he asked, smiling. He too had noticed the looks they'd been giving each other.

"Yesterday."

"Well, I'm happy for the two of you. I don't really have any rules about this here. You guys can be as open or as private about it as you want, as long as you respect the customers. But I have to warn you; if it ends badly, I'm not going to play favorites. If one of you causes a problem or can't work around the other, you'll have to go. I'm sorry, but that's how it is."

"I really don't think there will be a problem," Tyler said, glancing at Amy to see her nod in agreement. "We're both adults here."

"Of course. I just wanted to be sure I said it. You two have a good night and congratulations. And Randolph?"

"Yes sir?"

"Treat her right. She's a good girl."

"Of course, Doug."

The two of them walked to their cars hand in hand again, following a similar pattern as the previous day. Tyler drove to his house carefully, making sure he didn't lose Amy on the road. He checked his phone on the way, suddenly once again very aware his father hadn't called him back. Worry clouded his mind, causing him to almost pass his house in his preoccupation. He whipped his car into the driveway, giving her room to drive up beside him and stepped out.

"Do you want to meet him now, or later," he asked as she jumped out of her car.

"Now please."

"Right this way, dear."

He heard the dog whining from inside as he put the key in the lock, knowing he must have been lonely in a strange house by himself all day. The second the door was open his new friend was up in his face, licking his neck again until he noticed Amy. He bounded over to her with his tail wagging, ears flopping as he hopped. He sniffed her legs before jumping up and placing his front paws on her shoulders.

"I told you he was sweet. He has to belong to someone. He's too well-mannered not to."

"I see what you mean," she said as the dog put his nose to hers and chuffed in her face. "He's been taught to act this way, I'm sure."

"That was my thought. He's too friendly to be a stray and he seems house trained."

As if to prove this point the dog trotted out into the yard and lifted his leg on a tree near Tyler's porch. Tyler asked Amy if she wanted the tour now or if she'd rather wait. She gave him a sheepish look and said she'd love to wait if that was okay. They herded the dog back inside and climbed into Tyler's car.

"How old would you say he is," Tyler asked her as they drove towards the city for the second time in two days.

"I'm not really sure. Maybe a year or so. He still acts young."

I snapped a picture of him with my phone this morning. I'm going to make some flyers in the next couple of days. I don't want to spend a fortune on food just to have someone come and get him. Or worse buy something the poor guy doesn't like."

"You like him, don't you?"

"I do. I've always wanted a dog. I know it's only been a few hours, but he came in and made himself right at home. I feel like we kind of bonded."

Amy smiled at this as they drove, making more small talk as they discussed what to buy their new friend. They both felt that this trip was something that was also completely natural and both of them couldn't be happier.

"Since we're out again, would you like to get dinner? Or would you rather buy something and have me show off my chef skills?"

"We could cook. That would be fun!"

"Cook it is! Any requests?"

"I vote we check out the selection and see what catches our eye."

"Sounds perfect!"

They entered the supermarket hand in hand, loving the way it felt to be together. Their first stop was the dog food where they picked out a few cans of meaty varieties and a small bag of dry food. Tyler also picked up a few toys for the dog, whom they agreed to refer to as "Buddy" for the time being. As they made their way to the meat coolers they discussed their favorite meals, which were quite similar.

Looking over the selection they decided they would fix chicken breasts, sautéed chorizo and rice, their mouths watering as they planned the meal. As they checked out and drove back to Tyler's house the subject of their families came up again, Amy talked about her parents and sister who still lived in Virginia while Tyler avoided talk of his own family as long as he could. Once there was no more putting it off, he explained the situation as simply as he could.

"I've never been very close with my parents, "he said slowly. "I'm an only child and my father felt business trips were more relevant than sticking around to help raise me. Mom relied more on wine than anything to get her through the day. I never really felt at home in the world until I moved to the mountains. Now I feel like I have a solid hold on life and honestly," he said, taking her hand, "things are looking better by the day."

"You're something else," she said blushing. "Do you still speak to your parents?"

"Well," he began, thoughts of his father running through his mind, "I talked to my mother yesterday, but the relationship with my dad is difficult. I actually tried to reach him yesterday, too, but got no answer. I haven't actually spoken to him in three years."

"I'm sorry. If you haven't talked in so long, why did you try to call him yesterday? If you don't mind my asking," she said, terrified she'd overstepped some boundary.

"I had a weird experience earlier in the week and then I had a strange dream about him the night before. I guess it just weirded me out. Actually, the nightmare that woke me up last night involved him."

"Do you want to talk about it?"

"I don't want you to think I'm nuts"

"I won't, but if you aren't ready to tell me that's ok."

He told her he didn't have a problem telling her, and gave her a rundown of the events of the two dreams and his radio interference that started the whole thing. She remained silent for a few moments after he was finished. He had been vague about the more gruesome details so as not to make her think he was completely insane.

"Tyler, honey, I agree they're freaky, but they are just dreams, right?"

"I hope so. I feel like they've got a purpose, though. I'll feel better once I hear something from my dad. I hope you don't think I'm some kind of nut."

"Not at all. I've had my share of weird experiences. I get that they stick with you." They pulled into the driveway, Tyler feeling surprisingly comfortable to have shared this much with Amy.

They carried their purchases into Tyler's house and Tyler quickly readied a bowl of food for Buddy. As he was busy devouring his treat, they entered the kitchen together and began preparing their dinner. The process went flawlessly, both of them picking a task and sticking to it, creating a dinner that filled them up quickly, allowing enough extra for Buddy to find a few pieces of chorizo in his bowl the next time he returned to it. After dinner the three of them retired to Tyler's back porch, looking off the side of his personal piece of the mountain, the sky still holding a few brightly colored clouds as the sun's distant rays said their goodbyes for the night.

"This is a beautiful view," Amy said, laying her head on Tyler's shoulder as she moved closer to him on the bench the house's previous owners had left.

"I love it," he said, feeling his heart skip a beat as her body meshed perfectly with his. He didn't know if it was typical for two people to bond this quickly, but he knew that it seemed more normal than anything he'd ever felt.

They sat there until the sky grew dark, the first stars glinting in the night sky, watching as Buddy paced around the yard, sniffing the ground and marking his territory, never letting his new friends out of his sight. Tyler took Amy's hand in his, kissed her on the forehead and prepared to speak when he heard the growling start. He jumped, instantly seeing the wolf from his dream again, before he looked out at the yard, knowing he had to protect Amy.

"Tyler, what's wrong," she asked. "You act like you've seen a ghost."

She leaned up, finally hearing the growling and looked at his face before they stood up and peered out into the yard. They realized at the same time that it was Buddy growling. They could see him in the last remaining light, his haunches tense, hair on his back bristled as he looked at the edge of the forest and backed slowly toward the porch, growling as if ready to tear something apart.

"Buddy," Tyler whispered. "What is it, boy?"

The dog ceased his growling long enough to look back and give Tyler one quick tail wag before returning to his vigilant threat. As they watched the dog, questioning his actions, they began to hear a rustling coming from the underbrush. Tyler stepped forward, putting himself between Amy and the woods, telling her they needed to go inside. She took a step back, unsure of what Tyler was so worried about. The rustling got louder, driving her and Buddy to step back a bit faster. The dog growled deeper than ever, baring his teeth to the darkness. As she reached behind her to open the door a shadow burst out of the edge of the forest, drawing a little squeak of fear from her.

Tyler braced himself to protect Amy, hoping that she could get away before whatever it was in the darkness could get to her. The shadow leapt from the forest and hopped across the yard, darting around Buddy as he pounced forward. As the tall animal raced toward the other side of Tyler's yard he caught a flash of white as it flagged its tail, warning any other deer that may be watching to stay away. He laughed so hard he almost fell to his knees, suddenly feeling stupid for being so scared. He heard Amy giggling behind him and felt her hand on his back, prompting him to turn around.

"Well, that's deer two, you zero, City Slicker. You sure were ready to protect me, though," she said, sliding her arm around his neck.

"Of course. I'm not ready to lose you to some deer," he said, knowing this would make her blush deeper than ever. "But, you know, he could have just been warning you."

"Warning me?"

"You are planning on cooking his cousin in a couple days, after all."

She laughed again, pulling him down to her face and planting a kiss on his lips as they heard Buddy lope back onto the porch, joining their party by batting at their legs with his tail as he waited to be let inside.

"You never got that tour," he said, letting the dog go in and stepping aside so he could hold the door open for Amy.

"That's true. I think it's time I see where my protector calls home."

Tyler smiled wider than he had in a long time and followed the cute, petite blonde in the house. He pointed out the features of his own small house, one hand on her shoulder as he watched her reaction to his home decor. He was only a head taller than her, but when she looked up at him with her beautiful bright green eyes he felt like a giant. The tour of the downstairs ended with the living room, where she complimented his fireplace and the small portion of his book collection that was on display there.

When he asked if she'd like to see the upstairs she responded by grabbing his hand and pulling him up the wooden steps to the carpeted landing above. Buddy, more interested in his food dish, stayed behind for this leg of the tour.

Amy regarded his guest room with enthusiasm, the spare bed being nothing special, made at home in the midst of the boxes that lined one wall.

"I'm still kind of unpacking and rearranging," he said with amusement.

"I like it. It gives it a more developing feeling. Is there more to see?"

"Well, there's my room, and the attic. Let's go."

She requested that they go to the attic first, as it was closer to the guest room than the master bedroom. She became instantly enthralled with the fact that the house's previous owners had made the room into an office with a spare bed, which they'd left behind. Tyler had already placed a leather sofa in the room and kept a radio and lamp up there in case he ever wanted to try it out for a night. He could feel Amy's hand tighten around his as he led her to his bedroom and wondered what was going through her head. His own heart pounded, much as hers must have the day before.

"The only person who has ever seen my room besides me is the guy I hired to help me move," he said slowly.

"Good. Then I'll be more than honored to be the first unpaid visitor."

She entered the room slowly, looking around her in the last of the day's light while he turned on a lamp to shed a little more illumination on his small haven. Her eyes bounced across every surface of the room, pausing for a moment on the few pictures he had on display, the television on his dresser, and the closet door before resting for a few extra seconds on the bed. Tyler felt his breath hitch a bit as she walked over and sat on the partially made bed, inviting him to join her. Was she impressed? Was she nervous, too? What was going to happen next?"

He sat down next to her and looked into her eyes, seeing a look of deep satisfaction and interest coming from them. He leaned in and kissed her lightly on the lips, placing his hand on her lower back. She pressed back firmly, kissing him intensely as she ran her hand through his hair. They didn't say a word as their kisses became more passionate, Tyler being the first to allow his tongue to enter the equation this time. Amy pulled her legs onto the bed and placed her hand on Tyler's chest, pressing firmly to lay him back on the bed. Her hands found his shoulders and moved back around to his neck. Tyler let his own hands move down her sides, running his fingers over the swell of her breasts as he reached down to pull her leg up, feeling the warmth of her bare skin against his as her already short shorts rode up higher.

Their breath and saliva mixed as they kissed each other more frantically, both of their hearts pounding as their libido rose. Tyler felt her hands slide down and grasp the bottom of his shirt as he cupped her breast lightly. He moved up and allowed her to remove his shirt, waiting a moment before removing hers. She moaned a bit as he began to squeeze her breasts, his mouth moving down to kiss her neck lightly. Running his tongue down her neck, he kissed her breast softly, adjusting as she moved to climb on top of him. She unhooked her bra, tossing it aside as he grasped her hips tightly.

"Tyler," she said a little breathlessly. "I've never done this before."

"Good," he said, relief flooding his body.

"It is?"

"Very. I haven't either."

She smiled wide and kissed him again as they explored each other's bodies with a youthful urgency, feeling the passion grow with each passing second. Tyler paused and looked down into her eyes, feeling the soft, supple skin of her legs move over his as she readjusted to look into his eyes.

"Do you want to keep going," he asked her slowly, worried he was missing some sign in favor of one answer or the other.

"Do you?"

"I'm at your mercy. You're in control. We won't do anything you don't want to."

"It's been so amazing so far."

"It's been perfect."

"I don't know what to say."

"You can say anything."

"I want to keep doing what we're doing. But I want to wait to go farther. If that's ok?"

He kissed her deeply rather than answer with words and they held each other for what seemed like hours. They talked about their lives, what their childhood was like, how they felt and more.

"I think we should probably sleep at some point," Amy said with a sigh.

"Well, we do have to work tomorrow. And we have to be rested for mini-golf tomorrow night."

"Mini-golf?"

"If that's ok with you."

"I've always wanted to try that, but no one would ever take me."

"Well get your golf shoes, beautiful. I'm taking you right after work."

"I can't wait," she said before a look of questioning, almost embarrassment crossed her face.

"What's wrong?"

"Nothing really. I just...what if I'm no good?"

"Come on. You'll be great. Besides, I'll probably be terrible. I've got two left feet and I'm all thumbs."

"Ok. I do have a question."

"Shoot."

"Tonight..."

"Yes?"

"How should we spend it?"

"Well, I'd love it if we spent it together. You're more than welcome to stay here."

"I love that idea, but…"

"Do you have problems sleeping in a new place?"

"No, nothing like that…"

"Well, what is it sweetie?"

"I don't have any extra clothes."

"Oh, of course! I hadn't thought of that either. Well, as long as I leave plenty of food down and we stop in before golf tomorrow, the dog should be fine, so we can either crash here and stop by your place before work, or go back to your place tonight."

"Let's go say goodnight to him and sleep at my place. I'll bring extra clothes so we can stay here tomorrow if you'd like that."

"I'd love it," he said, kissing her again.

Buddy loped around the yard under Tyler's watchful eye while Amy put the rest of the leftover chicken in one bowl and filled another with dry food, giving him plenty of water as well.

"What if he uses the bathroom in the house," she asked when the dog came hopping back in, wagging his tail.

"Well, I hope he doesn't. I could run out before work and check on him."

"If it's a problem we can stay here."

"Actually, on second thought, maybe we should move his food to the porch and let him spend the day out there. That way if he does belong to someone he can go back if he wants. He seems happy here, but I don't want to keep him from his family."

"That sounds perfect. Plus that way we'll see if he loves it here like he seems to."

Gathering his bowls, they called him back outside, making a bed for him on the bench and telling him they'd be back. He seemed to understand perfectly, wagging his tail as they went back inside and locked the door behind them. With nothing left to stop them, the pair drove Tyler's car back to Amy's house and made their way to her bedroom. Once there, Amy guided him to her bedroom and sheepishly climbed into bed with him after changing into her night clothes. Turning off the lamp she laid her head on his chest and told him goodnight before going to sleep.

***

Tyler drifted off, listening to the sound of Amy breathing, feeling more at peace than he had in years. Without realizing he'd fallen asleep, he was dreaming. He found himself walking around in the old Douglas cabin, checking the door and the two windows, praying they were already locked. Amy sat in the corner, wide-eyed and trembling. He knew he had to protect her from whatever was outside. He tried hard to figure out what might be outside, remembering Buddy had already scared off the deer, and came up blank.

He threw a bolt on the door that he was sure had never been there before and walked to the fireplace to pick up a large knife that looked vaguely familiar. As he picked up the heavy blade, the moon slipped out from behind the clouds, illuminating the interior of the cabin and the fields outside. As the moonlight touched the floor of the cabin the howling started outside.

Amy whimpered from behind him, covering her head and shaking more. He lifted the blade higher, going to both windows, looking for the wolf he now knew was stalking them. He saw nothing. Amy was behind him, whispering a prayer or something under her breath. He wanted to comfort her, but refused to let his guard down. He couldn't let something get to her. Not now. Not after he'd finally made a connection with her. He walked through the cabin, waiting for another howl, knowing he had to be ready for an attack from any angle at any time. He only hoped his blade was big enough. He would have to get much closer with this than he did with the branch, he knew. But that was a dream, he thought, pausing mid-stride. Why would I think about that here? This is life.

He walked back to the window as a second howl rang out from the other side of the cabin. Amy whimpered, jumping like she'd been shot. Tyler ran to the other window, catching sight of a large black shadow as it darted around the corner. He ran to Amy, kneeling before her and grabbing her arms. It was only then that he realized what he'd thought was a prayer was something worse. Amy was whispering to herself the same thing over and over again.

"We shouldn't have gotten out of the car. We should have stayed."

"Amy," he whispered, shaking her a bit, bringing her back to the present. "You have to be quiet. You can't make a noise. It's close. We can't let it know we're in here."

She nodded, too terrified by what he told her to do anything else. He stood once more, facing the two windows, waiting for the wolf to burst through one of them, ready for the kill. He would not be caught unawares again. He didn't know how it had found them, but it would not get to Amy. Not this time. What was he thinking? Not this time? He glanced back at Amy, finally noticing the dark band around her calf, recognizing it as his own bandana, glowing a deep blue in the moonlight. What had happened? He was almost too scared and angry to try to remember.

He heard claws drag across the wall behind the fireplace and braced himself. He waited to see it walk by one of the windows, listened intently for another sound from outside, but heard nothing. He was just about to walk to the window nearest him when it happened. The thing must have run with all its might at the cabin wall. As he stood there waiting, something slammed into the wall behind Amy hard enough to rattle the door in its frame. Neither was expecting this sort of attack and Amy, scared and shocked already, screamed out when it happened. The thing now knew where they were. It howled in triumph and fury after hearing her scream. Slamming itself against the walls over and over, the wolf growled so loud it rattled the windows in their frames. Amy crouched in the corner again, whining. Tyler saw the tears rolling down her cheeks and knelt to comfort her, telling her they would get out of this.

The wolf stopped thrashing the walls of the cabin as he said this, the growling subsiding a little as he heard it walk around the cabin, scratching the wooden walls as it did. He faced the windows as he heard it dragging its claws on the wood of the cabin walls, waiting to see it peer in at him angrily. The scratching stopped as it reached the wall behind the fireplace again, the growling turning into one long, mournful howl that threatened to deafen him. Tyler covered his ears as the howl went on and on, seeming like it would never stop. Amy's cries were drowned out by the howl. His chest rumbled with a new sensation, confusing him until he realized that it was a growl. The wolf was still howling outside, so it couldn't be that. This must mean there were two of them. Tyler gripped his knife tighter than ever, terrified that he wouldn't be able to protect Amy after all. The sound grew louder as the howl outside subsided, the rumbling affecting his breathing, quickly becoming all he could hear. Before long the growl was mixed with a ripping sound that he couldn't identify. As he realized this, he also noticed that the sound of Amy's crying was gone. She must be terrified beyond belief, he thought, whirling around to comfort her.

Nothing he had seen or dreamed in his life could prepare him for what he saw. Amy, the woman he had finally begun a normal, adult relationship with, was all but gone. What remained was a large creature that was even worse than what he had imagined happened to his father. Where Amy had been lay a large, blonde creature that was writhing and twisting, its face- Amy's face- a mask of pain and hatred. As he watched, the skin of her legs split open, blood spilling out, exposing the leg of a large blonde wolf, covered and matted in the blood of the woman he'd come here with. Her painted toes stretched to match those of the creature that he'd seen his father turn into. When this horror was complete her hairy, canine arms ended in a cross between a hand and a paw with two inch claws covered in blood and flesh, gleaming with a visceral newness in the moonlight. Her face was the last to go, her beautiful green eyes flashing once before beginning to glow with some inner light that he didn't understand. He heard the sound of something hitting the floor and looked around before realizing that the sound was coming from the Amy creature. He watched closer, realizing to his horror that the sound he heard was her teeth being forced out of her mouth by the growth of jagged, bloody fangs. The she-wolf reached up and ripped what remained of Amy's face off what lay below, the flesh he had so recently caressed landing in a bloody heap at his feet.

The furry snout of the wolf elongated, the fangs all sliding into place as the rest of its body reached a stage of completion. It reached down, ripped the clothes off of its new frame and stood on all fours, shaking itself like a wet dog. Blood and bits of flesh were thrown around the small cabin, splattering on every surface as Tyler was soaked by it. Completely changed, the she-wolf turned to him, keeping him in sight with those bright green eyes, and began to growl fiercely, causing the wolf that was now watching from the window closest to Tyler to howl once more. As he looked over to see the black wolf looking at him in what looked like a state of triumph, the thing that had been Amy leaped forward, knocking him to the floor. The she-wolf crouched on him, her front paws pinning his shoulders down as he struggled to reach the knife that had clattered less than an inch from his outstretched fingers.

"Amy," he said pleadingly, "are you still in there?"

The she-wolf snapped her jaws closed just inches from his face, spraying him with a mix of blood and saliva as he tried to get the one thing that could save him. She put all her weight on his right shoulder, digging her claws into it, as she pushed his bones to the point of popping his shoulder out of socket. She raised the other paw above her head in a gesture that he understood instantly. She meant to slash at him, maybe tear out his throat, maybe even take his head completely off with those claws.

"Amy, please. Don't do this."

His pleas did no good, he knew, as the she-wolf flexed the muscles in her raised arm, her snarl getting louder as hatred shone forth from her eyes. He didn't know how, but in the moment before her hand dropped, he heard her voice in the growl, saying the one thing he'd been trying to avoid realizing this entire time.

"This is your fault, Tyler. You did this to me. We should have stayed in the car. You should have been honest with me. Now I'm a monster, and you aren't going to live beyond tonight."

The she-wolf's paw swung down in an arc and slashed at Tyler's chest. He felt the white-hot explosion of pain cover the front of his body. She lowered her head and licked the blood from the wounds, seeming to grin as her eyes met his, her body shuddering as she tasted him. Tyler felt his stomach churn as the pain filled his body. She slashed at him again, this time catching the side of his face as he turned his head away. Her hot breath coated his bleeding skin as she licked him again, her body tensing as his blood ran down her throat. He chanced a glance upward as he felt her breath quicken, watching in fear as she opened her jaws wide, leading him to do the one thing he knew he would never be able to forgive himself for.

Thrusting the knife upward, he pushed the blade between her ribs, feeling her flesh cut like butter. A scream that was more human than he expected filled the cabin, making him want to join it. He forced himself to bite his tongue as he removed the blade and pushed it into her stomach, feeling her claws dig into his shoulder as he fought desperately for his life. He felt the wolf on top of him grow heavier as she weakened, her blood now pouring freely over Tyler's body as he tried to get out from under her. Using the last of her strength she looked down at him and darted her head forward, wanting to take him with her as her life faded. He moved instinctively, bringing the knife up and shoving it into her mouth, through the top of her snout before he even thought about it. Her body fell limp on his, her life seeping out of the wounds that he caused as tufts of hair fell from skin that was fading to a pale white once more. He watched as the wolf's body shrank back into that of the woman that had been taken from him. He couldn't take his eyes off the knife that protruded from the top of her skull, his hand still gripping the hilt that was pushed into her open mouth. Amy's eyes met his as her body became human once again, her breath hitching once as her eyes both thanked and blamed him for the last night she had spent on the earth. He was stunned at first. Had this actually happened? He shook Amy slowly, knowing it would do no good. He had killed her. He had really killed her. As this realization sank in Tyler couldn't hold his scream back any longer.

He awoke in the darkness, covered in sweat, the sound of his own voice waking him up. Amy sat up beside him, holding the sheets up to her chest, looking at him in alarm.

"What's wrong? Tyler, sweetie, what is it?"

"Nothing. Thank God. It's nothing," he said, swinging his feet to the floor and dropping his sweaty face into his hands.

"It's something, Tyler. Most people don't just wake up screaming outside of the movies, honey. Come on."

"I had a nightmare. The worst one I've ever had. But it's over now. I just…"

"Just what," she said, hugging him back as he turned and threw his arms around her.

"I'm glad you're ok."

"Of course I am, why wouldn't I be?"

"These nightmares. They're not just random. I mean they are, but they're connected somehow. I don't know how. I don't understand it, but I know, or I think, it's got something to do with my father."

"Talk to me, honey. I'm here for you. You can trust me."

"OK. Just please don't think I'm crazy. Hell, I might be, but just let me believe I'm not. Let me start from the beginning again," he said as he looked into her beautiful green eyes, kissing her once before he told her everything that had happened in the last three days.

***

Amy sat in silence, mulling over what Tyler had just told her. His nightmares seemed a little severe, but not crazy to her, but they had impacted him deeply. She knew whatever she said next could either greatly help, or severely hurt him.

"So I was a wolf?"

"Well, I don't know. It's like it came out of you. Like it ripped you open, like I said."

"The same way it did your father?"

"Not exactly. He just changed and turned. With you it was like it literally came out of you. Like one of those old space alien movies."

"And it attacked you?"

"Yes."

She thought for a few more moments, staring out the window at the moon, just now rising behind the mountains.

"You think I'm crazy."

"No, actually. I think this whole thing is coming from hearing your father's voice. That's when it all started."

"But why the wolf?"

"Well, you said you heard a coyote outside your window that first night."

"Yeah. But the second night? Tonight?"

"The second night you woke up and heard Buddy panting. Maybe that was even him the first night. Dogs howl, too."

"I actually hadn't thought about that. Maybe I heard him growling at something, too. He sure went after that deer tonight. But it still doesn't explain why I just had that dream."

"I would say a combination of leftover trauma and confusion about the other two dreams mixed with…"

"With what?"

"Well, with feelings…you are having some feelings, right?"

"Absolutely, "he said, lying back on the bed, rubbing her back. "I guess that could really be it. All because of some radio interference and a dog."

"And a woman, of course. Don't forget the problems we cause," she laughed as she lay back down her head on his chest again as she looked up into his eyes.

"Problems? You could never cause any problems, doll face. You're too cute."

"I'll keep that in mind, handsome. Do you think you can sleep better, now, or do you need to stay up more?"

"I think I'm good."

"Good. Because I need to get my beauty rest, or you'll stop looking at me the way you do."

He laughed, "Never."

They drifted off again quickly, both of them smiling as they held hands, feeling the now familiar warmth of one another's bodies. Tyler didn't have another nightmare that night, but every dream he had seemed to leave him feeling like there was something watching him. As the moon rose higher, it's pregnant, pearly light showing that it was nearly full, neither of them heard the howl in the distance.

***

They awoke at around 8 the next morning, feeling refreshed and happy. Tyler knew this was exactly what he needed in his life when his first sight that morning was Amy looking back at him. She smiled as he awoke, kissing his cheek as they both stretched.

"Morning, "he said as he brushed her hair behind her ear.

"Hey there, handsome. How'd you sleep?"

"Great. How about you?"

"I had a dream that I had an amazing night with this guy and when I woke up this morning he was still here."

"Is that so?"

"It is."

"And what happened next?"

"Well, I got up and stepped into the shower. I offered to let him join me, but I woke up before I found out what he decided. I guess now I'll never know..."

"You know, you could always just climb in and see what happens."

She laughed and climbed out of bed, taking his hand and leading him to the shower. The two of them cleaned up, washing each other as well as themselves and got ready for work together.

"You know," Tyler said as they ate a breakfast of toast and cereal, "Kayla may have a heart attack when we show up in the same car."

Amy laughed into her bowl, admitting that that was probably true. They left together, arriving at work about 20 minutes early. They were the first ones there, so they opened the office up and started a fresh pot of coffee, checking the box for the two small local newspapers and cracking them open to check each one for a missing dog ad while they waited for Kayla and their boss. Amy flipped through her paper quickly, not paying much attention to anything while Tyler carefully examined the headlines of his, unsure if he was wanting to find one or not. They switched when they were done, Tyler looking through Amy's paper with the same vigilance he'd checked his own. He saw nothing about a missing dog, but one headline caught his eye.

Man attacked, found dead beside car.

Tyler skimmed the article quickly, not knowing what he was expecting, but feeling there were many details left out. According to the reporter the man's wife had awoken that morning to find her husband wasn't in bed. She vaguely remembered him telling her he'd heard something outside, but couldn't remember if he came back in or not. The man's body was mangled so badly the police just assumed an animal had attacked him, but had released enough information for the article to be written. The house in question was just 30 minutes from the tour area, and less than an hour from his home. The only other details were the man's name and more comments about his wife. Tyler laid the paper down slowly. Could this have anything to do with his dreams? He knew bears attacked people occasionally, and knew warm spells in the winter like this could confuse them and make them active early, but would a bear mangle someone that badly? Animals were about as unpredictable as people, he knew, no matter how much they were studied, but it bothered him. He smiled at Amy, telling her he supposed Buddy was safe with them for at least one more day if he hadn't gone anywhere. He didn't mention the article to her, feeling he'd already burdened her too much with his problems as it was. Most women would have bailed on him after hearing a story like that, but not Amy. He had known it from the beginning, but the more time he spent with her, the more he could tell that she was different. He grasped her hand as they both stood to get a cup of coffee, hearing the sound of a vehicle pull in from outside.

"That'll probably be Doug," Tyler said, pulling a third cup from the cabinet as Amy agreed, knowing their boss was definitely a coffee man.

The door opened slowly, Kayla walking in and glancing around before whistling at them.

"I only see one car out there," she said in a matter-of-fact tone, a smile on her face.

"Yeah," Tyler said, both of them blushing a bit.

"So things are going well, I assume," she said as she walked over and hugged Amy.

"They're going great," Amy said as she stepped back.

"I'm glad. I'm really happy for you two. You're good people."

"Well thanks, Kayla," Tyler said. "Have a cup of coffee with us while we wait on people to show up."

"I don't mind if I do. You've already broken into the papers, I see, unless Doug has been here and left."

"No, it was us. We were looking for an ad."

"Oh? Already looking for a place or something," she said, laughing a bit as they sat down at the table together.

"A dog, actually," Amy said, winking at Tyler.

Kayla coughed on her coffee as she looked at her friends with wide eyes. "Are you serious? You've been together for two days and you're wantin' a dog?! Come on, now."

"She's kidding," Tyler said, explaining the situation with Buddy and why they were looking in the papers.

"Well, getting a dog is one thing, but if fate decided to send you one, that might not be so bad. What kind is he?"

"He looks to be a German Shepherd. He's pretty big, mostly brown with some black around his face and paws. He's pretty protective of us both already."

"He is?"

"Yeah, he warded off a deer last night while we were sitting outside with him."

"Sounds like he's a good dog to me. Someone may be missing him bad. But then again, someone may have dropped him off."

"We left him outside last night in case he wanted to go back home."

"Did he?"

"Well, we don't know…"

"Too busy to check this morning," she asked laughing a bit and winking at Tyler.

"We actually went and stayed at my place last night," Amy broke in, seeming to be growing more comfortable talking about it with Kayla.

"Oh, fair enough then. You know, it could be that that dog didn't have a happy life. He might have run away from wherever it was he lived before and came to you all to take care of him and keep him safe."

"Do you think we shouldn't put up flyers, then," Tyler asked, finding this possibility interesting.

"I would go with your gut on that one. If you feel you should put some up go ahead, but I would watch whoever comes looking for him. See how he reacts to them and how they treat him before you just hand him off to someone who tries to claim him. If he did come to you for love, you don't want to put him back in a bad situation."

They heard cars pulling into the parking lot as they agreed this would be the best way to handle the situation.

Finishing their coffee, they walked outside to greet whoever was waiting. They found three customers who were eager to take their little tour, all standing in front of the ticket window that hadn't yet been unlocked. It was just after ten and Doug never kept the window shut past 9:50, they all knew. Looking out into the parking lot they didn't see his car anywhere. Kayla stepped aside to call him while Tyler and Amy went to apologize for making the customers wait, and explain that the boss hadn't arrived yet. Kayla came back and gestured for them to come with her.

"He didn't answer his cell or his home phone," she said, worried. "I've known that man for more than ten years, worked for him for five and I've never once known him not answer a phone call. I've got a bad feeling about this."

"What should we do," Tyler asked as another car pulled into the lot, this one carrying a young couple that used their window to announce their recent nuptials.

"I've got a key to the office so I can go ahead and sell tickets to these folks. You two can give the tours this morning and I'll work here until lunch. If Doug isn't here by then I'm going to his house."

"OK. If you need anything from us just let us know. We'll take the tours and everything. I'm sure Doug is fine," Tyler said, hoping he was right.

Tyler and Amy gave three tours that morning, switching who was in the lead each time, always meeting in the back to herd everyone back down from the cave at the end of the tour and make sure no one was left behind, enjoying the walk hand in hand, often smiling at other couples and newlyweds that came to tour as they did so. It wasn't until the last tour that Tyler saw the piece of trash by the side of the cabin, remembering that he and Amy hadn't brought their stuff down from the day they'd eaten on the porch. As Amy let the tour group explore the cabin he walked over and grabbed the empty sandwich bag, wadding it up in his hand and pocketing it. He was turning to walk back to the front of the cabin when he noticed the mark on the wall. It was subtle, but obviously new. It was about three feet in length and consisted of four scratch marks that were about hip height to him. Crouching down, Tyler spread his fingers wide and ran them over the mark, making a perfect fit. He could barely hide his shudder as he ran around the cabin and joined the group, hoping Amy wouldn't ask him where he'd been.

***

Doug still hadn't arrived when the lunch hour rolled around. Kayla, clearly worried, drove to his house to check on him as she said she was going to. Amy asked Kayla to call her the second she arrived and especially let them know if anything had gone wrong. Tyler watched Kayla pull away before turning to Amy and telling her he needed to show her something.

"Are you sure they haven't been there before," she asked when he showed her the marks on the cabin wall.

"I'm positive. You see how white they are? That's the mark of fresh cut wood. Look," he said, picking up a gravel from beside the porch and making a vertical scratch above the others. "Once it's been there awhile the sun and the weather will make it go darker and match the rest of the log."

"Could it be a bear?"

"Bears do mark their territory sometimes, but why here? And are bear paws this similar to a human hand," he asked, running his fingers down the length of the scratches again.

"I don't know, honey. What else could it be?"

"I'm not sure…"

"Are you suggesting that some kind of monster did it?"

"No. Not necessarily."

"Tyler, the thing you've been dreaming about is just that. A dream. There are no men that turn into wolves."

"The Cherokee had legends of men that could become animals and the other way around."

"They also had legends that the trees would talk to them if they spent three days starving in the woods. There are no monsters here."

"Maybe. But I have a bad feeling about Doug."

Amy agreed on that aspect of the conversation as Tyler walked around the rest of the cabin with her to see if there were any more scratches on the walls. The search same up empty, prompting them to return to the break area, where Amy excused herself to the restroom. Tyler put his hands in his pockets, feeling the plastic sandwich bag. Pulling it out, he started to throw it away when he noticed that it looked cut. He examined the bag, seeing two marks running right down the middle of it that he knew weren't there the day they ate the food. He quickly stashed the baggie in a drawer that no one used, feeling certain they were claw marks.

Kayla called when she arrived at Doug's house, reporting that he wasn't there and no one answered the door. She couldn't find a spare key anywhere to allow her to go inside, so she was at a loss on how to react. She came back to the office, looking defeated, having decided that if Doug hadn't shown up or called by closing time that she had no choice but to call the police and report him as a missing person. None of them had seen him since they'd left at 5:30 the day before and that was very unlike him. Tyler and Amy covered the tours for the rest of the day, having only one group come in, winter seeing the tourists start to choose indoor activities rather than quaint hikes, even on the unnaturally warm days like this. It gave Tyler and Amy plenty of time together to discuss their night, deciding they wanted to have a nice small dinner before going to play mini-golf. Conversation faded as quitting time came and there was still no sign of their boss. Kayla asked them to stay with her while she made the call and they gladly obliged, the three of them sitting around the table in the small kitchen area again. The police told Kayla they would begin a sweep of the area within the hour after hearing that it had been almost 24 hours since anyone had seen or heard from him, telling her that if nothing came up by morning they'd want to speak to the three of them.

"I guess there's not much to do but wait," she said as she hung up the phone. "If he contacts either of you, please let me know."

"Of course. I'm sure he's fine. He probably had a family emergency and we're the last thing on his mind. He'll get in touch. Don't worry," Tyler said.

"Tyler's right. You know Doug's mom hasn't been in the best of shape lately. Maybe he's just taking care of her. Didn't he tell us cell signal is bad at her house?"

"I think so," Kayla said. "I'm sure you guys are right. I'm just a worry wart. Thanks for sticking with me and helping so much today. Now get out of here. Go have a good night. Tell the dog hello from me."

"I forgot we have to check on him," Tyler said. "We probably should be getting to that, in case he's out of food or water."

They left, saying goodnight to Kayla as she locked up and walked to her car. The drive to Tyler's house didn't take long, his foot growing a little heavy on the accelerator in an effort to get away from the cabin quickly in case whatever made those scratches was watching them somehow. Amy's car sat where she'd left it in Tyler's driveway, as they'd expected. Climbing out of his vehicle he whistled once, hearing a little bark from behind the house followed by the sound of big paws hitting the ground. He steadied himself against the car as this sound still brought him chills after his dreams. Buddy soon appeared at the corner of the house, one ear flopping lazily as the other one stood up in a state of alert. He stopped running and stood in the yard, tail wagging and tongue lolling. In that moment Tyler and Amy both would have sworn he was grinning.

"Come on boy," Tyler said, clapping his hands.

The dog bounded forward and jumped up, almost knocking Tyler off his feet and covering him with hot, sticky saliva. His attention waned as Amy walked around the car and he left Tyler to give her an equally slobbery greeting.

Laughing they wrangled him back onto all fours and set off for the house, Amy subtly carrying her bag of clothes over one arm as they went in to wash their faces before going out. Tyler opened the door and stepped aside to let dog and woman inside first, Buddy going straight to the back door and waiting patiently for Tyler to get his food and water dishes, both of which were dangerously low. Buddy had eaten the chicken and licked that bowl clean and eaten all but a few bites of his dry food. The water, complete with a few blades of grass and a dead fly was little more than a puddle in the bottom of the bowl. Tyler filled both bowls generously and carried them back outside for the dog, who had settled himself back on the bench to rest. After Tyler and Amy washed their faces they stepped back outside to play with Buddy for a minute before getting back on the road to prepare for their third date in a row.

***

The night went great. They had dinner at a small short order diner, complete with a jukebox that played some of their favorite Golden Oldies. They finished their dinner by sharing a malt, both of them feeling the sense of false nostalgia their city was famous for providing its visitors and loving every second of it. Mini-golf went better than either of them expected, Amy beating Tyler by two strokes. As the winner, Tyler told her, she had the honor of choosing their next destination. She wanted to take a walk by the river and look in a few souvenir stores, to feel like a tourist for a night, she said. This sounded perfect to Tyler, who was ready to do anything he could to keep the smile on her face. They ended up sitting in the grass at the river's edge, staring at the reflection of the nearly full moon on the water and feeding the ducks and fish handfuls of food pellets from a quarter machine nearby. They looked at each other seriously after laughing at the ducks squabbling over the meager feast and both knew what they felt, though neither felt ready to say it aloud. They let their lips do the talking as they listened to the rushing water and the sounds of the city as life went on around them, both forgetting they had a care in the world as they lived only in this moment.

After buying a bottle of soda from a small store, they made their way back to Tyler's car, the clock registering ten once more as they discussed where their next destination should be.

"It's still the lady's choice," Tyler said, taking a drink of the soda and offering the bottle to her.

"I think," she said, taking a sip and suppressing a small hiccup, "that we should go back to your place."

"That sounds perfect to me," he said, navigating through the thick late night traffic.

They entered the mountains as the moon was rising to its highest place in the sky, pearly white light illuminating the road ahead. Soft rock music played while Amy held his hand, making Tyler's heart flutter a bit with a combination of giddiness and nervousness. He couldn't help but be reminded of the moonlight from his dreams as the shimmering light moved over the ground like a living creature. As he rounded a curve his headlights reflected in what had to be the largest pair of eyes he'd ever seen. Glinting yellow-orange in the artificial light, the eyes seemed to both enrapture and frighten them both, Amy letting out a soft gasp. He slammed on his brakes, sending his car skidding sideways, nearly going off the road and into a ditch. They watched as a large, thick shadow broke itself off from the edge of the road, the slow, ambling walk clearly that of a bear. The squat, waddling animal crossed the road, giving them one more cursory glance as if laughing at their reaction, and ambled down over the embankment and into the brush below.

"Tyler," Amy said slowly.

"Yeah, honey," he said, turning the wheel and slowly straightening the car out before continuing towards his house.

"Are you ok?"

"Yeah. That just startled me. I thought…"

"You thought it was something else?"

"I wasn't sure. I just knew I didn't want to hit it."

"It's probably a good thing you didn't."

"It would have caused a lot of damage to the car, but I wouldn't want to hurt the bear either."

Amy smiled, satisfied with his response, and went back to looking out the window, watching the stars through the thick trees above. She didn't see him wipe away the one tear that spilled from his eye or feel the pounding of his heart in his chest. He had no idea how she couldn't hear the latter, as it almost deafened him even over the music coming from the speakers. For an instant he was certain that the thing from his dream had found him in real life. He took a deep breath after they rounded the next curve, knowing they would soon be coming up on his driveway, which in his mind was somehow infinitely safer than anywhere else they could be.

The rest of the road offered no surprises and they were soon comfortable on his back porch while Buddy inspected the yard, looking up to make sure they were safe every few minutes. The moonlight shone on the ground, casting light shadows as the breeze blew leaves over the ground. They laughed as Buddy would see one that he was particularly interested in and would chase it, throwing it up and biting it out of the air before it had a chance to touch the ground. The romantic nature of the atmosphere was not lost on the two young lovers, who soon entered an embrace that the world let them have. They kissed deeply, paying no mind to the dog that was now creeping slowly towards the woods, hair on his back raised, growling deep in his throat. The sound was carried away on the wind before it reached them. They went on, undisturbed, oblivious to the eyes at the edge of the darkness that watched them, unblinking. As the dog approached, the eyes turned to look at it, driving a blade of icy fear into his heart. Crouching low to the ground to show submissiveness, Buddy backed up slowly, aware that he was barely hovering above the product of his own involuntarily emptied bladder.

The eyes in the forest turned away as the dog reached the porch, their owner receding into the mountains as silently as it had appeared. Buddy turned and ran up the stairs, running to his water bowl and drinking heartily in an effort to calm down his beating heart.

"Buddy," Tyler said over the dog's lapping. "You sure know how to ruin a moment, man."

Amy laughed her beautiful laugh and kissed Tyler on the cheek. "You're just thirsty, aren't you boy," she said, reaching down and ruffling the fur of his neck. The dog wagged his tail in reply, still drinking water like he had just spent weeks in the desert.

"Do you want to stay out here or go inside," Tyler asked as she turned back to him, smile more beautiful than ever in the moonlight.

"We can go in. To your room, if you want," she said shyly.

"I think that sounds great."

They entered his bedroom much as they had the night before, Amy in the lead, turning the lights on as they entered. Tyler cracked the window to get the breeze inside as Amy lay on the bed, her stomach full of butterflies. Tyler joined her soon and they continued where they left the night before, stripping each other's clothing off quickly, pleasuring each other slowly. Amy requested that they still not take the final step, feeling their present situation was already at such a level that she wasn't sure if she could handle more. They lay down together, both feeling exhausted and ecstatic.

"Amy," Tyler said, his hand cupping her cheek as she looked at him.

"Yes, sweetheart," she said, loving the way he looked at her.

"I'm really glad I met you."

"Me too, Tyler. I'm really glad you kissed me."

"I've wanted to do that since the day I met you."

"So have I. I was just too shy to even do more than think of it."

"So was I. I just couldn't hold myself back anymore. And I'm glad I couldn't. These last few days have been great."

"They really have. You know how to show a girl a good time. You've made me feel like a visitor in our own city. I don't know how you do it."

"Oh," he said, laying back, "it's that northern charm."

She laughed, pulling his face back to her and kissing him hard before asking if he felt like sleeping. She turned out the light when he said he was fine with that and told him goodnight, snuggling to his chest as their naked bodies intertwined beneath the sheets.

"If you have a nightmare, or you need anything in the night, don't hesitate to wake me up, OK?"

"You've got it, babe."

Tyler laid in the dim room, the moonlight seeping in anywhere it could find a crack, rays of light falling all across his floor with the fluid quality he'd always been fascinated by. He looked down at Amy, her beautiful face looking peaceful as she slept. He kissed her forehead gently as he listened to her slow, steady breathing. He had known more happiness with this woman in three days than he had felt in the vast majority of his life. He had no idea what would happen in the future, or even the next five minutes, but he knew that whatever it was, he didn't want to have to face anything without her by his side. He thought she had been having similar thoughts, and as he drifted off to sleep he found himself hoping that she felt that same way he did.

Tyler slept for a long time without dreaming, his body relaxing completely as he and Amy shared the same bed for the second night in a row. The moon had traversed the entire sky and was quickly approaching the horizon again, the eastern sky just showing the first hints of light before his mind slipped into what, at first, seemed more of a memory than a dream.

He was young again, sitting in front of the television, his mother somewhere in another part of the house, paying him no mind. She was likely with his father, whom he seemed to remember had walked in stinking, barely looking at him. The smell had remained long after his father had walked out of the room. It reminded him of the older kids in gym class and at the same time kind of like the neighbor's dog after he'd been out in the rain. The cartoons on the television seemed unusually violent to him today. As he watched, not only did his favorite cartoon rabbit angrily maim his duck friend, but the normally goofy coyote seemed much more menacing as it finally caught the bird he was always chasing, biting the poor thing's neck before stomping on the body and walking off screen.

Tyler stood up, suddenly not feeling comforted by his favorite cartoons right now, and decided to find his parents and see if they would play a game with him. His mother usually said no, but his father almost always said yes. At least he did if he wasn't sick. His dad wasn't around much. Tyler supposed he went to the doctor a lot, because he usually left around the time he wasn't feeling well. Tyler always knew when his dad was feeling bad because he got grumpy and hungry. It hadn't happened often around him, but there were a few times his father had been angry with him for doing silly things that his mother didn't care about, like watching scary movies. As long as they didn't bother his sleep, his mother let him watch one every now and then. His father always made him stop, saying there were enough nightmares in real life without making up new ones.

He strolled through the living room, looking around him, loving the small house that he lived in. As he entered the hallway he heard his parents talking. It sounded like they were angry again. He hoped they weren't, but he knew they fought a lot these days. Usually his presence would make them stop. As he walked toward their bedroom his mother raised her voice to a new level, demanding that her father take something evil away from the house. He heard a pained response and then what sounded like his father crying and asking for help. He heard the sound of a slap, so loud it made him jump and then everything changed. He heard his mother gasp as the sound of growling filled the small hallway. He thought for a second that his father might have brought him a pet as the growling grew louder, something definitely beginning to feel wrong. This thought was driven out of his head as he heard a thump, followed by a scream from his mother. This isn't what's supposed to happen next, he thought, somehow slowly realizing that things had changed from how he remembered them.

Tyler found himself walking toward the door and tried to stop. He told himself that this was wrong. He had to run, even tried to physically make his legs stop moving, to no avail. He had no choice but to watch in horror as his hand reached out and opened the door of his parents' bedroom. The first thing he saw was his mother lying on the floor, her head turned to the door, mouth and eyes wide in an eternal scream of terror and pain. His eyes then caught the largest thing in the room. The hairy black figure leaned over his mother's corpse, devouring the inside of her chest as warm blood gushed out of wounds in half a dozen places on her body. As he watched, unable to move, the thing turned to him, blood and entrails hanging in thick ropes from its jowls and growled. He was frozen to the spot as the thing left his mother's body and began creeping toward him. It was a little over a foot away before he finally began to back up slowly, not knowing what was happening, but knowing that his mother was dead and this monster had killed her. Was this what his father meant? Maybe he had watched one too many horror movies and he was just having a nightmare. He tried to shake himself awake and had no luck. He knew that something was off here, but was unable to pinpoint what it was. There was something oddly familiar about this monster, about this whole situation.

As he watched, looking at the thing still creeping towards him, something about the scene changed. At first he couldn't tell just what it was. The monster was still bearing down on him and he was still clearly a child. It wasn't until his eyes darted away from the creature that he realized what it was. The body in the bedroom floor was no longer his mother. It was Amy.

Tyler awoke in the darkness, panting a bit, feeling the adrenaline flowing through his body. He hadn't screamed at least. As far as he could tell Amy was still sound asleep, her body pressed against his, making him warm and instantly more comfortable. This dream had been very different from his others. His father was still involved, but it had been so strange, so unlike anything that had actually happened. His parents had fought a lot, but to his knowledge neither had ever struck the other. He had certainly never been stalked by some evil wolf monster in his parents' house. The sun had begun to rise outside the windows, its rays peering through the blinds much as the moon's had the night before. Looking at the clock, he realized that it was just after 7. He adjusted himself a bit so he could reach his phone, seeing now that they both had notifications, the indicator lights blinking in unison.

"Amy," he whispered, brushing her cheek. "Wake up, sweetie."

"Hmm," she mumbled, opening her eyes and smiling as she saw him looking back at her. As she realized he was what had awoken her, concern filled her sleepy eyes. "What's wrong?"

"Nothing, I hope. We just have messages. I just noticed the lights blinking. It might be Doug."

Tyler grabbed their phones and handed Amy's to her, looking at his own screen to see that, in fact, the message had not been from Doug, but from Kayla. Amy voiced the same realization as he opened his own string of messages from her, of which there were four. Amy had received 5, all of them increasingly alarming. Apparently Kayla had gone back to Doug's after work to search for him again, to no avail. She had passed police cars on her way and there had been one parked near his house, apparently watching to see if there was any activity nearby. The next message was a bit confusing, saying she had found him. After this Kayla had apparently lost her mind. As far as they could tell, Doug had been killed in an accident at some point, a fact that made their stomachs hurt.

"Should we call her," Amy asked as the realization of what she'd read sank in.

"I guess we need to. These messages are a few hours old."

Amy sat up, dialing Kayla's number as she did, putting the phone on speaker so they could both talk.

"Hello," Kayla said after the third ring. "Amy? Are you OK girl?"

"Yeah, Kay, Tyler and I are fine."

"He's there, too?"

"Yeah, you're on speaker."

"Hey Kayla," Tyler said softly.

"I'm so glad you two are OK. I was worried something had happened to you. I'm sorry to disturb you. I just needed to tell someone and check on you guys."

"You're fine, honey," Amy said quickly. "Just tell us what happened."

"I'd rather tell you in person."

"We can meet you anywhere."

"Just come in to work for a bit. The police want to talk to us all anyway."

"OK. We'll be there soon."

"I still need to shower. God do I need to shower. I still have it on me. I just...Just meet me there at regular time. OK?"

"Sure Kay. Whatever you want. See you at ten, honey."

Tyler and Amy stared at her phone for a moment, unsure of what to do or say.

"What do you think happened," Tyler said slowly.

"I guess we'll find out at ten?"

"Yeah. Come here," he said, wrapping her cool, naked body in his warm embrace.

They waited a few more minutes before climbing into the shower together, repeating their procedure from the day before in Tyler's slightly larger shower, going to his kitchen after dressing in their underwear. They ate omelets and toast for breakfast, trying hard to make the most of a bad situation. As they cooked breakfast they danced around the kitchen, their own feelings for each other bringing them out of the funk they had slid into. They knew their boss was gone, and they hated the situation, but their own pure happiness just at being in each other's company made the pain easier to bear. After they ate they stepped out to check on Buddy, Amy worried about someone seeing her in her underwear.

"Well, if anybody watches, they've already caught an eyeful from me. I don't really have close neighbors, as you can see. At most you'll have some deer ogling your goodies."

"Just deer, huh," she said, laughing as his eyes slid down her body again.

"Well, it's a given that I'm going to look. All men are pigs. Didn't you know that?"

"Oh, how feminist chic of you, Mr. Randolph."

"I'm always here to defend the weak," he said, winking at her when she played offended.

The dog heard their laughter and hopped down from his bed on the bench as they opened the door, his tail wagging heartily as he licked their hands, unsure if he should jump on them because they looked so different. They filled the dog's food and water dishes and played with him for a bit. Tyler went into the yard and threw a stick for him until he started panting in the late winter warmth.

"Come on and lay back down before you get too hot, pal," Tyler said, climbing the porch steps and sitting next to Amy. She had her arms and legs crossed trying to make sure that as much of her as possible was covered in case there was someone watching. They kept the dog company for a few more minutes, feeling bad for leaving him unattended so much, before telling him they'd see him the next day. They hurriedly got dressed, Tyler grabbing some extra clothes for the night after making sure Amy was OK with that plan.

"Yeah, I want you to spend the night. I think we should drive our own cars, though. In case the police are weird."

"That's fine."

They gathered their belongings, locked up the house and left in their own cars, both dreading what they would find out once Kayla arrived. Tyler let Amy lead the way, cruising along behind her, listening to his favorite rock station to keep his mind from wandering too far in the wrong direction. They arrived at the office before Kayla, unlocking the door and starting the coffee again. They made small talk that mainly consisted of the menu for the night, the plans for the weekend and what they thought the police would ask. Kayla's car entered the parking lot, taking the spot closest to the office that they'd left for her. She came into the office, her eyes still bloodshot, fresh tears spilling down her cheeks when she saw them.

"I was driving along the road," she said after she'd calmed down. "I had already driven it once, so I didn't think there would be anything there. I had already passed the cops on the way to his house and I just didn't think anything of it. I came to a wide place, you know, one of those pull offs that are like unofficial overlooks? Well, my phone went off and," she broke into sobs again, her voice cracking as she tried to go on.

"Shh, Kay," Amy said, "take your time. Just calm down."

"I'm OK. I just can't believe it. Anyway, my phone went off. It was a social media notification. It told me that Doug was nearby. The shared location thing, you know? He's asked us all to do it in case one of us gets lost in the forest and all. But anyway, it told me he was close. I was so shocked I stopped in the middle of the road. I didn't see anyone or anything coming in either direction. I didn't know what it could be, so I did all I could think of. I pulled over and got out."

"On the highway?"

"In the wide patch, where everyone gets out. I stepped out and looked around me, waiting to see him drive up and wave that wave of his, but I saw nothing. I walked up to the edge of the gravel and saw it. The weeds didn't even show where it happened, it was just down there."

"What was, Kayla," Tyler asked slowly.

"Doug's car. That's why the phone had gone off. It had picked up his phone. I called the cops and they came flying down the road in minutes. There was a crane there in half an hour, pulling his car out. The paramedics had tried to get to him… but it was no good. He was thrown out. They said it looked like he went through the window and slid down the mountain, and at some point the car rolled over him. His body was scraped and mangled like crazy. They said…," she held up her hands, indicating that she needed a minute. Tyler went to the fridge and got her a bottle of water, giving her time to take a drink and calm down.

"They said he was barely recognizable as a human."

"Then maybe it wasn't him?"

"It was. I saw the clothes. That's all they would show me. I saw the clothes, the car and his phone and wallet. They're going to try to check dental records to be 100 percent positive, but I'm sure it was him. I could feel it, you know?"

They did. They consoled her as best they could, asking her if there was anything they could do. Their discussion was cut short by a knock on the door, and Tyler opened it to find two police officers standing there.

"Officers, please come in," he said, nodding at them in turn.

"I'm sorry to barge in on you folks," the senior officer said. "We just have to ask a few questions, and I wanted to come extend my personal apology and explain what we know so far."

They all understood and asked the officer to proceed.

"Well, first off; do any of you know if Mr. Morris had any family to speak of? We've been unable to track down a next of kin."

"I don't know that he has much," Kayla spoke up. "His father died years ago and his mother is homebound. She has dementia. I think he was an only child. He never married and never spoke of children of other family."

"Alright, thank you. Did Mr. Morris ever say anything about being depressed or unhappy at all?"

"No. Not at all," they all said in unison.

"He was always one of the happiest people I'd ever met," Tyler said, taking over. "You can tell when someone is genuinely happy and when they are putting it on for show. Doug never does that. Did that..."

"Alright, finally, had any of you had any altercations or disagreements with Mr. Morris in the days before his death?"

"Absolutely not," Amy said at once. "Doug wouldn't fight with a man who was trying to steal his wallet, just lean up and hand it to him."

"Fair enough. I think those are really the only questions you all can help us with. Now, since this case is a bit unusual, I would like to tell you some of what we know," the senior officer continued, while the younger man stood with his hands behind his back, watching closely.

"Mr. Morris, while on his way home Tuesday night appears to have left the road for one reason or another. Upon leaving the road, his car was thrown off the top of the mountain ridge. At some point during this event, Mr. Morris was ejected from the vehicle. Once the car and Mr. Morris came to a stop, he was badly injured. Our team thinks he died on impact with the mountain, but until a full autopsy has been performed, we can't be totally certain. Being in the mountains, it appears that something made it to what was left of Mr. Morris before we did. Our initial exam shows signs of an animal attack. Thus far it appears to have been post mortem, but again, we aren't certain."

They had all remained silent during this exchange of information, but Tyler, terrified of what he'd heard, spoke up first.

"What sort of animal do you think it was?"

"We aren't certain yet. Unfortunately, we aren't sure it's prevalent to the investigation either way."

"Understandable. If I may ask one more question," he said, catching Amy's eye as she hinted he should stop.

"Ask all you'd like, any of you."

"Well, how can you be sure the man you found was Doug?"

"Well, his possessions for one. The man we pulled from the ravine had Mr. Morris's wallet and phone, complete with multiple calls from all three of you. Furthermore, Mrs. Davis has been so kind to identify the clothing he had on that day. I understand those things aren't strong, but we have been able to get some dental impressions and we are currently working to check those against his records to be certain we have the right man."

"Thank you for being so thorough," Kayla said, her voice cracking, though she looked slightly more composed.

"Of course. You understand that what I've told you is largely confidential. As I said, this is an unusual case and we needed every bit of your help we could get."

"Excuse me again, Officer," Tyler said, knowing he was pushing his luck. "I know you're investigation is incomplete, but what do you think happened?"

"Well, off the record, my own opinion is that we may never actually know. I think he was driving and for one reason or another something caused him to swerve in the exact wrong place, sending him right over. Judging from the direction the car travelled in after its initial impact we do think he was going in the direction of his home. Unfortunately, I'm afraid that's all we know. We are very sorry for your loss," he said as stood up, gesturing for the other officer to go to the door. "I think, until we are able to track down some information on his next of kin and what we should do with this spot, it may be best to close down for a few days. I am very sorry about that, but it may be best."

"We understand," Amy said, with a note of sadness in her voice. "Thank you all so much."

The officers apologized again, the younger one saying his first and only words for the entire encounter, and left. Tyler and Amy turned to Kayla, who was still sitting at the table, looking sadder than ever.

"Close the office? How could we open it? What else do they expect?"

Tyler and Amy didn't know. Kayla didn't want to stay in the kitchen much longer, either, asking them to walk her to her car.

"I think I need a break from the mountains for a few days," she said as she reached her car. "I'm going to go home today and sleep and then I'm going to go to my parents' for a few days."

"OK, Kay. We understand. You and Doug were good friends. You need to be able to mourn."

"Sweetie, we were more than friends once. We were lovers. That's why I knew so much about him. I loved that man with all of my heart, and he loved me. We just couldn't make it work in a normal way. I just need to be away from it all to process it. I love you, girl, and I'll let you know when things are easier. Bye, Tyler. You take care of her, OK?"

"Of course. You be safe, Kayla."

"I love you, Kay. Please be in touch. I'm going to text you often, OK?"

"Sure sweetheart," she said, climbing into her car and pulling away quickly.

Tyler and Amy returned to the office to lock up. They glanced at the papers for that day, not really paying much attention to anything in them. After a few moments they turned off the coffee pot, Tyler wishing at least one person had had a cup, knowing Doug would have sucked the carafe dry. They walked slowly away from the building after locking up, neither sure what to say. It was barely after 1 in the afternoon and both were trying hard not to think too much of their former boss. Tyler, despite knowing he had nothing to do with it, couldn't help feel that he was in some way responsible for the man's death. He left last every day, but the fact that he actually insisted Tyler and Amy go on and let him lock up made Tyler feel he'd somehow done something wrong. He could tell by the look on Amy's face that she also had a similar feeling.

"Well, what should we do today," he asked her slowly.

"I thought we had a date?"

"We do, if you're still up for it. Do you still want to go to your place and cook and everything?"

"It sounds good to me. I want to cook you a good country meal, you city slicker," she said, forcing a smile to go along with her teasing.

"Well, I do love getting some culture," he teased back, winking at her.

The tension eased immediately once they began talking again. The pair leaned against Amy's car and talked for a few moments, deciding they would go to her place and find something for lunch and watch a movie, Amy confessing that she wasn't sure she could handle being alone and telling him again that she loved being with him. Tyler, feeling the exact same way, thought for a moment of telling her that his feelings were developing to new levels. This was interrupted by a car pulling into the parking lot. As they pulled into a spot two kids shot out of the back like bullets, the little girl doing cartwheels behind the car while the little boy plucked early dandelions from the grass and threw gravel into the weeds, both trying to relieve the tension of sitting in the car, wasting their youthful energy.

"I can't handle this," Amy said, looking to Tyler, her eyes suddenly very full of grief again. "Can you take care of them?"

"Sure, babe," he said, walking over to the family as the father got out and approached the office.

"Good morning," the man, a nice working class guy, said when he was close enough to Tyler. "Have you taken the tour?"

"Actually, I'm one of the guides," Tyler said, letting the man get a little farther from his family before breaking the news to him. "Unfortunately we aren't open today."

"Oh no, why not," the man said, seeming genuinely disappointed.

"We've had a bit of trouble today."

"The kids and I were really excited about seeing the cavern. One of their friends did the tour last summer and that's all they've talked about since. I travel a bit, and I'm not home as much as I'd like, so we become sort of explorers whenever we have the chance," he explained.

"I understand," Tyler said, suddenly finding it hard for him to explain the situation.

"Is there any way you could give us just a quick look?"

"I'm sorry, but we just aren't able. You see, our boss, the man who runs the center, was found dead last night."

"Oh Gosh! That's terrible! How did it happen?"

"The police aren't sure. For one reason or another he swerved off the road sometime before yesterday morning. They found his car last night at the bottom of a ravine."

"Oh my," the man said, guilty relief flooding his features. "For a second I thought you meant he died here. Either way, that's terrible. I'm very sorry for your loss. Were you close?"

"I hadn't known him all that long, but we were good friends. My coworker is taking it pretty hard," he said, nodding back towards Amy who had climbed into her car as Tyler approached the family.

"I understand. What happens next?"

"We're going to close here a few days, give the grief time to settle, go through with the funeral and all and hopefully we'll open back up sometime in the next week."

"Alright. We'll come back before we leave next week and try again. I'm sorry for your loss. You all have a blessed weekend."

"Thank you. I hope you and your family have a great vacation."

The men shook hands and returned to their respective sides of the parking lot to give the rundown of the encounter to their parties, Amy dabbing her eyes as she noticed Tyler returning. He told her things were fine, looking up when he heard the cry of disappointment from the children as the father herded them into the car, throwing a wave Tyler's way as climbed in himself. Tyler returned the wave, dropping the hand back down to wipe a stray tear from Amy's cheek as he bent down to kiss her.

"Let's go back to your place and get our minds off of this. We've got a lot of fun ahead of us this weekend, right?"

"Absolutely," she said, as if she needed the reminder that he was going to be by her side as they dealt with this loss.

He climbed into his car and followed out of the parking lot, his mind full of worry. What would they do for work now? If Doug didn't have a will, who would get ownership of the cabin and cavern? Would whoever it was keep them on or fire them and hire his own crew? For that matter, would they be dedicated enough to remain open year-round and offer winter cavern tours so the guides would remain employed? As these thoughts rolled through his mind, he heard the radio in the background begin to break up a bit. A voice came through for a split second, reminding him of his father. He turned up the music, half expecting to hear the command that he should stay in the car again. As he listened, two stations fought for dominance on the frequency, as they usually did in the mountains. One voice shot out above the others before his rock station came back full swing. It hadn't even been a full word, but Tyler was certain that the voice was saying something about a cabin.

***

He chose not to say anything to Amy about this latest experience, halfway believing it was just his imagination making something out of nothing anyway. He trotted up to her car and opened her door for her once they got there, bowing slightly as she laughed at him and praised him for picking up the charm and courtesy of a true Southern gentleman. They walked into her house hand in hand, fixing a quick lunch of salmon and fries before settling down to watch a comedy to put themselves into a better mood. Laughter filled the house as they watched comedians try to navigate their way through a foreign country after a night of heavy drinking. They were cuddling on her couch, their minds free of the stress of the day when Amy looked at Tyler and asked him if he had ever had anything like what they were currently experiencing.

"Not even close," he said honestly. "I've had a few girlfriends, but that mostly consisted of awkward dates and even more awkward first kisses. I actually only got past the first kiss with two girls besides you."

"Why?"

"Different reasons. Either the girl said she just wanted to be friends, or just that we shouldn't date. Once I even heard, through a mutual friend, that I was just creepy and she was afraid I might get clingy if she talked to me anymore. And I've ended a couple of would-be's myself."

"Wow. That's very harsh. What about the ones you ended?"

"Well, one of the girls was a smoker. The kiss tasted like I was licking the ashtray in my neighbor's old Buick. And with two, I guess I was a bit shallow."

"Weren't they pretty enough?"

"Oh no, they were pretty. They were just absolute morons. One girl literally asked me why clouds don't fall out of the sky if gravity was so strong."

"Seriously?"

"Oh yeah. She was a piece of work."

"I'm almost afraid to ask where she is now."

"Last I heard she was working at a clothing store, selling shoes and perfume. What about you?"

"Well, most recently I've worked at a tour center," she said, smiling at her snarkiness.

"Very funny. You know what I meant," he said, tickling her ribs, pleasantly surprised when she wiggled and laughed out loud.

"OK. You don't have to get so rude! But no, I've never had anything even close."

"You're beautiful, though. You must have had guys asking you out constantly."

"Well, I was a nerd in school. I wore glasses, had braces until sophomore year, and kept my nose in the books. But once I navigated through puberty and shed the braces, I was noticed a bit. Unfortunately it was just jocks."

"Most girls would have loved to have jocks falling over them."

"I hated it. They always came up and asked if I'd like to be their lucky date after the football game on Friday, usually saying something along the lines of how I could even be their good luck charm. One even told me if they won he'd let me ride him like a stallion and tell anyone I wanted."

"Charming guys."

"Top of the line, that's for sure. But that's life in a small town. The old folks worship football players so they think everyone else should, too. Especially women. Of course, most high school girls did. From what I hear they still do. The guy who made me such a generous offer?"

"Yeah," Tyler said, wondering what was coming next.

"Last I heard about him he had just fathered his fourth kid from three different women and was flipping burgers at a fast food place."

"Such high aspirations."

"That's how some people are, though. They peak in high school and the rest of their lives just don't compare. It's sad, really. That's why I had to get away. I was tired of seeing my friends get caught up in drugs and guys and ending up either in jail, pregnant or on welfare or some combination of the three."

"That sounds rough."

"It's not all like that. For the most part people actually do go on and succeed. As a matter of fact, one of the guys I graduated with just got voted into a political office in Idaho. I didn't mean to play into the stereotypes like that, but I guess I see why the news does it. It's easier to remember some of the worst stories than it is to see the best."

"I know what you mean. My best friend growing up, well...my only friend for one year... first grade was rough. Anyway, he was put in jail for selling meth just before I moved down here. It's not just small towns that have the bad seeds. Believe me."

She felt comforted just listening to him talk. Her mind had been plagued by the idea that he was the kind of guy who did this often, seducing women with his innocent act just to leave them once he'd played them fully. After hearing him talk, however, Amy was certain Tyler wasn't that type of man. His eyes told the story of someone who was just as new to these feelings as she was, a fact which made her feel much better with their current situation. She'd never felt the way she did about Tyler before, and it was honestly a bit scary, but she knew if she waited it out, if could prove to be an incredible journey.

As if he knew what she was thinking, Tyler kissed her passionately, making her practically melt. She kissed him back eagerly, the pair beginning to make out like kids at a school dance as they explored their feelings as well as each other's bodies. Amy pulled herself down, sliding under Tyler as he lay with her, his hands sliding down her body and resting at her hip. It stayed there for a long time, its heat and weight driving her crazy, making her more turned on by the minute. Just when she thought she couldn't stand it anymore he moved it up, grasping the bottom of her shirt and pulling it off almost before she knew what was happening. She took his off as well, loving the way his skin felt against hers as they continued to kiss.

She slid her hand behind her back, unhooking her bra, wanting to feel more of him against her. He took it off and threw it to the floor, kissing her chest before standing and picking her up. As she looked at him in awe, unsure of what was coming next, he carried her to her bedroom and lay her on the bed, climbing in after taking his pants off, now wearing nothing but boxers. She contemplated for just a moment before she took off her own shorts, taking her underwear with them, getting Tyler's off as well. She reached into her night stand and pulled out a condom from the box her mother had sent her a month ago, suddenly happy the woman was delusional about her love life.

"Are you sure," he asked her, unable to hide the swell of his manhood as it pressed against her.

"I am. If you are."

He kissed her in response, waiting a few moments before putting it on. The experience lasted longer than she expected, and felt greater than she could have imagined. She knew Tyler was new at it as well, but the way their bodies worked together, she felt they were meant to have the experience together. After it was over they lay in the deepening dusk, both of them happier than they'd ever been, the shock of the experience having tired them out more than they expected. Amy was dozing when she heard Tyler move, saying her name as he adjusted to look into her face.

"Yes," she said, hoping that he would say what she couldn't.

"That was incredible."

"It really was. I never knew it would be like that."

"I don't think it usually is."

"What do you mean?"

"I think, for some people, it's a very different thing," he said, clearly struggling to get his point across.

"How so?"

"Well, some people just go out and do it with anyone and everyone they can. Other people...wait until they find someone...."

"Find someone?"

"Yeah. Someone they, you know, care about."

"I think you're right."

"You do?"

"Absolutely. If you do it with a lot of people, then it really doesn't feel special. Right?"

"Yeah," he said, his brow furrowed as he lay his head back.

Why won't he just say it, she thought to herself before realizing that it was probably for the same reason that she wouldn't. She was terrified to be the first to say it, halfway expecting him to either say he didn't feel the same way or just not say anything at all. But would that happen at this point? She was certain they'd both been feeling the same way the entire time they'd been together, even though it was just a matter of days, but after hearing what he said about the experience itself, she felt positive that Tyler felt the same way she did.

They lay in silence for a bit longer, loving the way their bodies seemed to fit together perfectly, Amy's head on Tyler's chest as they relaxed. In those moments, nothing else in the world mattered. To them, nothing existed beyond the edge of the bed in which they'd both just bared their souls and given themselves to the other. This reverie was broken by the sound of Tyler's stomach growling loudly in the silence. They both laughed at this as they realized they hadn't checked the time since before they came to the bedroom. Evening was coming quickly, the sun outside low on the horizon. It was after 5, so they decided they would go down and fix dinner and watch another movie while they ate.

Their night was one they wouldn't soon forget. Amy prepared venison the way her mother and grandmother had taught her, a recipe that had been passed down from generations before them both. Tyler found himself quite pleased with the meat that he'd watched Amy prepare with careful but practiced hands. Amy was pleased with his satisfaction, feeling that she had made a very good choice in introducing him to her family recipe. They ended up watching two movies before retiring to Amy's porch swing to watch the moon rise through the clouds. The night was eerily silent, both of them noticed, and the breeze seemed to hold a chill which had nothing to do with the remaining winter ahead. As the moon rose through the clouds, peeking its pregnant head over the mountains, they realized that it was larger than they'd ever seen it. It looked huge, its orange tint throwing a brownish blanket of light onto the clouds around it. As it rose higher, a red cast began to creep across it, making the night sky seem to glow a deep maroon that made chills run down their backs.

"I've never seen a moon like that," Tyler said slowly, looking around him, half expecting to see a dark figure emerge from the shadows to come take them to Hellish places the likes of which they couldn't imagine.

"I have, once," Amy said with a shiver. "I think it means there is an eclipse. I took an astronomy class in high school. We had to watch an eclipse one night and the moon turned red like that for hours. It definitely wasn't that big, though. I kind of want to check the news and see if something weird is going on."

They decided to check their phones to look for any story relating to the current state of the lunar occurrence. Tyler hit gold first.

"It's the Wolf Moon. And there is an eclipse, making the red color they call a blood moon. They're calling this a Super Blood Wolf Moon, because it's one of the moon's closest passages to earth. It hasn't happened for nearly 20 years apparently."

"That's actually kind of interesting."

"Yeah. Of course, there are people who say it means terrible things are coming. A lot of people actually believe it means the world is going to end."

"That's a comforting thought," Amy said, feeling a chill that she knew wasn't caused by the wind. "Are there any happy theories about it?"

"Well, scientifically speaking, it won't happen again for almost 20 years, if that counts."

"It's a start."

They put their phones away, sitting in silence as they watched the redness spread, almost a quarter of the moon consumed by the creepy, albeit natural phenomenon. Amy drew herself closer to Tyler, feeling comforted as he put his arm around her shoulders. No cars passed in the darkness, the silence so loud it seemed to press in on them. They realized at the same time that the sounds of the night had ceased, if they had ever been there at all. The night before there had been night birds and other sounds of nature that made the night seem comforting. But not tonight. The wind blew through the dead leaves that clung hopelessly to branches which would soon drop them for new growth, creating a sound that reminded her of something being drug through the dead foliage. She imagined a huge shadow lumbering through the woods, dragging the body of its latest victim behind it. She shivered as she imagined that it was the wolf from Tyler's dream, creeping around her house, bringing his nightmares into reality.

"Are you ok," he asked as he felt her shiver and tense under his arm.

"I just-," she began before being cut off by her phone. She looked at the screen and saw Kayla's face, hoping for an instant that her friend was calling to tell her that the body the police had found wasn't Doug after all.

"Hello," she said, after a nod from Tyler. "Kayla?"

Tyler could hear the sound of hysterical crying coming from the small speaker. He couldn't make out the words, but the longer Kayla spoke the more Amy sat up, growing rigid and seeming terrified.

"Honey, calm down. I don't understand. Doug was there? And what about your dog?"

She listened to the story again, nodding as if Kayla could see her through the phone before saying the only thing she could think of that would help solve the issue. "I'll be right there. Just stay inside, Kayla. Calm down." She nodded a few more times before hanging up and turning to Tyler.

"We have to go to Kayla's house."

"What's going on?"

"She's having a terrible fit. I don't know if she had a nightmare or what. She told me that Doug had come to her house and killed her dog."

"What the hell?"

"I know. She said she walked outside and found her dog dead on the porch. His throat had been ripped out."

"Seriously?"

"That's what she said."

"Well why does she think it was Doug? Doug's dead."

"She said he never liked her dog. The first time he came to her house the dog bit him or something. I could barely understand that part. She was hysterical."

"Well what's the plan?"

"We need to go see what's going on. If nothing else we have to make sure she doesn't hurt herself."

"If her dog has really been attacked then it could be serious. Buddy doesn't have anywhere to go for protection."

"I know. If you want to you can go and check on him and then meet us at Kayla's."

"Will you be safe going out there by yourself? What if there really is something out there?"

"She has a gun, and so do I."

"You do?"

"Of course. Do you think my daddy is going to let me live alone without a way to protect myself?"

"Fair enough. If that's what you want to do, we'll get on it. You could just come with me and grab the dog and we all go to her house."

"I want to get there as soon as possible. She's thirty minutes from here, you're twenty in the opposite direction. By the time we went to your house and then to hers it would be over an hour. I don't want her alone that long."

"OK. Let's get going. I don't want you alone that long either."

They grabbed their keys from inside and ran to their cars, kissing each other before they parted. Tyler asked

Amy to be careful, feeling a bit more comfortable as she placed her gun in the passenger seat beside her. He backed out first, burning out as he raced toward his own house, unwilling to let Amy spend more time alone than necessary. He knew he was going too fast as he went around the curves, his back tires sliding off the road and into the gravel. He felt the pull of the rubber as it caught on the edge of the road, but pressed the gas pedal harder rather than the brake, only slowing down when he approached his driveway, whipping the car in and leaping out without turning off the ignition.

"Buddy," he shouted, running around the back of his house, fearing the worst already. "Buddy, are you OK boy?"

He heard only silence from the back of the house, seeing nothing as he rounded the corner. The moon overhead was now almost halfway eclipsed, casting an ominous red glow over the dew covered backyard. He started the flashlight app on his cell phone, turning the bright light to the ground, fearful one of the wet patches he saw was actually blood. He leaped onto the back porch, his footsteps like gunshots in the silence and was immediately thrown to the ground as a large animal emerged from the shadows and slammed into his chest. He was certain this was the wolf from his dreams, made reality somehow by the terrifying moon. He was kept at bay by the deep growl coming from the animal on his chest, his breath ragged and painful against his suddenly very dry throat. He shined his light toward the creature, determined to look his attacker in the eyes if he was going to be another victim. His light shined into the face of the dog he'd come to check on, sending a flood of relief to his body.

"Buddy, you silly dog, get off of me," he said to the still growling animal.

Recognizing his voice, the dog underwent an immediate turn around, his growling stopping to be replaced with whines. He felt the dog begin to wag his tail as he backed off to let Tyler stand up.

"Are you OK, boy," he asked, reaching down to pet the dog's head. "I got a little worried about you. I was going to take you with me, but I think it might be best if I leave you here. Kayla's torn up about her own dog and I don't want to make her feel any worse."

Grabbing the key hidden above the door frame he opened the door, quickly transferring the dog's bowls to the kitchen and filling them before checking the doors and windows in his entire house. He approached the front door, wanting to get to Amy quickly when his phone rang. It was her.

"Are you OK," he asked immediately.

"I'm fine. Are you?"

"Nervous as a jack rabbit, but I guess so."

"Is Buddy OK?"

"Yeah. He scared me pretty good, but he's OK."

"Thank God. This is bad, Tyler."

"What? Kayla?"

"She's a bit better now, but the dog... the throat wasn't just torn out, the head was ripped completely off. I've never seen an animal attack like this. He didn't look like he'd been eaten or anything. Just attacked and left to bleed out there. Almost like something, or someone, wanted Kayla to find him."

"That's terrible. I'm sorry you had to see it. Is there any sign of the attacker?"

"No. Not that I could see. Her yard is just grass, so there wasn't really anywhere to leave footprints."

"You have your gun, right?"

"Yes. Do you have one?"

"No. But I've got some knives my dad gave me."

"Please bring one or two. I don't want you getting caught without a way to defend yourself. If this was a person, they're absolutely disgusting. If it was an animal...I really don't know what else it would do."

"I'll grab something. I was actually just about to leave. I'll be on my way to you in five minutes."

"Be careful. Don't drive out here like you did before. Once you pass my house the road gets bad. Take the second right after you get past my driveway and stay straight. Her house is the only one with a mailbox at the bottom of a long driveway."

"I'll be careful. I'll call you if I get lost."

"You won't have service for about 15 miles. Once you get onto Kayla's road service fails until you get a little ways into the forest and start climbing again."

"OK. I'll remember. I'm going to grab a knife and be on my way."

"Are you bringing Buddy?"

"No, I thought it might upset her more."

"I actually hadn't thought of that. You're probably right. There's no point in pushing it. Just be careful."

"You've got it, babe. I'll see you soon."

After they hung up he ran to his room, thinking of the large knives his father was insistent he should have. He looked through the boxes, pulling out the biggest two he could find, finally choosing a large dagger that was one of the sharpest in his small collection. He remembered his father saying that it was an old blade that had been forged in another country and brought over by an early settler. His mother had thrown a fit, telling her recently-estranged husband he'd basically just given a twelve-year-old the equivalent of a sword before he could he even shave. The blade itself was made of a fine metal, covering the length of his forearm from hilt to tip, the handle adding an extra four inches to the overall length. It felt good in his hand, he realized as he ran down the stairs, threading his belt through the sheath and letting the light weight rest on his hip.

He locked his front door, saying one more goodbye to the dog and closed it behind him, running to the car that was still idling in his driveway. He adjusted the dagger so it was easy for him to grab should he need it while driving. He threw his car into gear and left, burning out again as he rocketed back up the road toward Amy. She had asked him to go slow on after he passed her house, he knew, but he was going to make up every second he could between their houses. He raced up the mountain, his back tires slipping off the road with every turn, his engine wide open and roaring in the darkness. As he reached the edge of one curve he almost barreled straight into someone travelling in the opposite direction, both of them swerving and barely missing clipping each other in the darkness. He heard the sound of their horn long after he had rounded another curve and kept going. Had he not seen them continue driving in his rearview mirror he would have been tempted to go back, but he knew he had to get to Amy. He passed her house in a rush, slowing down until he reached the second right turn.

He braked until he'd pointed his car in the right direction and pressed the gas again, knowing that Amy had said the drive should take around 30 minutes. He had made the trip to her house from his in about 12 minutes, shaving off 8 of the usual 20ish, so he knew he could do better. As he rocketed down into the valley he remembered that he had promised her he would be careful. Not willing to break a promise to someone so important he stepped off the gas a little, slowing down slightly as he approached a curve in the road. He braked a little harder than normal as he started around it, realizing what Amy meant when she'd warned the road was dangerous. The curve bent around the face of the mountain until the road was almost touching itself, forcing him to slow to what felt like a crawl as he went through almost half a dozen more turns just like this. He sped up a bit more once he reached the bottom of the mountain, the road leveling out in front of him.

As he drove a little faster he was taken aback as he shot into a clearing, open fields on either side of him as the night sky shone overhead, the now three quarters red moon looming in the forefront, an inescapable danger he was both enthralled and terrified by. He could barely keep his eyes off the moon as he drove, having to correct himself a few times as he ran off the road, once coming within a foot of sending the nose of his car into the deep ditch, carved over the years by the redirected flow of water that ran along the right side of the road. He forced himself to keep his eyes on the road as he approached a long, subtle curve, the end of which revealed the edge of another section of forest, the ever reddening moon leering overhead. His eyes were drawn skyward again as he approached the trees, making him drift to the right once more.

He dropped his eyes back to the road and corrected himself, turning the wheel quickly, feeling his heart skip a beat. As he adjusted his wheel and attempted to calm his heart a large, hairy figure ran across the road less than a yard away from him. Tyler panicked and swerved to avoid hitting the creature. His car left the road and went straight into the ditch. As he swerved he slammed on the brakes, his car screeching to a stop after he left the road, his front bumper lightly tapping the bottom of the ditch. He sat in the car, feeling the breeze blow in his open window, frozen in place. His hands gripped the steering wheel so tightly his knuckles were practically glowing white. He breathed deeply, his heart hammering in his chest as adrenaline flowed through his veins. He gradually regained his composure as his heart slowed, his hands relaxing once he realized he was beginning to lose feeling in them.

"OK," he told himself, trying to calm down. "I'm not dead. I'm not hurt. I just need to start the car and see if I can get out of here."

He turned the key in the ignition, hearing the abused engine cough and sputter to life with chagrin. He popped the car into reverse and lightly pressed the gas pedal, hearing fuel dump into the engine. The car went nowhere. He pressed the pedal harder, hearing at least one of the tires spinning, throwing gravel from the small creek bed into the grass nearby. After trying a third time, he decided to see if he could go forward and gain any more purchase that way. It was no good. He was hung up. He would have to try to fix the problem another way. He turned the car off, taking a deep breath and deciding to relax before taking any further action.

He wondered what had crossed the road in front of him as he rested his head against the back of his seat, feeling stiffness setting in for his tense neck and back. He hadn't hit the bank hard, so he knew didn't have whiplash.

"Thank God for that," he said in the darkness, rubbing his neck.

He replayed the scene as best he could, trying to remember the animal. All he had seen was a large, hairy black shape. He knew it was either on all fours or running very hunched over. The animal had looked to be around 4 or 5 feet tall, taller than any bear he'd ever seen on all fours. He began to panic again as his brain immediately went to the monster from his dreams. Could it be that the thing he'd seen was some man, wolf monster? No. It couldn't be.

Tyler stopped thinking and decided to listen to see if he could hear anything outside. Expecting to hear growls and howls from all around, Tyler heard only the wind. The sporadic rush of the night breeze blowing the leaves around was a welcome sound, but he was again confused by the lack of other normal night noises. Maybe his crash had upset the animals and insects in the area, causing them to go quiet until they knew he was gone. But he couldn't go anywhere just yet. He couldn't get his car out. As he halfway listened for the sounds of the night, his brain filled with an image of the beast from his dream, saliva dripping from its terrible fangs as the moonlight reflected in its eyes. He was brought back to reality by the sound of movement in the field. He jerked his head forward, hearing the whisper of movement again, the sound of something moving through the brush slowly, to avoid detection. He grasped the handle of his dagger, hoping the sound was just another deer.

Silence filled the night again, the occasional gust of wind the only sound he heard. He looked all around the car, expecting to see a shadow darting or bounding across the road, or even through the fields, but saw nothing. The wind continued its sporadic blowing as he looked around, realizing he may have just made it up. The sound he heard could have just been the breeze blowing a little harder, or in a different direction. He had almost convinced himself that such was the case when he heard the sound again, this time coming to him over the wind. He looked around him again, seeing nothing. As he peered out of his window he heard the sound of scraping along his trunk, as though someone were keying his car. He whirled around, looking into the night and seeing only road. The red moon continued to illuminate the night enough for him to tell that nothing was in the road or standing close to his car. He gripped the handle of the dagger tightly as he imagined the thing from his dream circling his car, trying to find the best way to get to him.

He waited for another sound, knowing that he was being hunted. The time crept by. He looked at his watch, looking all around him, certain he had been waiting for hours. It hadn't even been ten minutes. He grew more impatient with each passing second. He was sure he was being toyed with and he refused to let his guard down. He had his weapon, it was a little before one in the morning, and he was very eager to get to Amy. She had said he would be out of signal for around 15 miles. He knew he had driven at least half that. He checked his phone to be sure there wasn't signal, finding Amy had been right.

In high school he had been able to run a mile in about four minutes. If he had eight miles left to run, he figured he would have to run for about half an hour straight, more or less. He knew it would be difficult, but at this point he didn't see that he really had another option. As he mentally prepared himself for the challenge, his father's words came back to him.

"Don't get out. Stay in the car."

Could this be what he meant? Could his father have been attempting to somehow warn him of this very event? No way. That couldn't be possible, could it? His mind had just created all of these things, like Amy told him. He'd let himself believe that his father's voice had come to him over the radio and now he was driving himself crazy. More than likely all he'd seen was a bear, or even a deer. As fast as the whole thing had happened, who knew if he even remembered it right? It could have been a bear running across the road and his mind had interpreted it as something else. Stranger things had happened, he knew. But what if he was wrong? What if the dreams were some kind of premonition? What if his father had really been warning him against this wolf monster and it had finally come into his life and put him in the very situation his father had warned him about?

As he thought about these things the sound of movement came to his ears again, coming from the passenger side of his car as best he could tell. What if there was a wolf? What was it doing? Worse, what would it do if he got out? He remembered the way his father and Amy had been changed in his dreams, the image of the she-wolf ripping Amy's face off to reveal its own making him sick to his stomach. His father had told him to stay in the car, so he should just do that. He could be patient enough to wait until morning. Besides, someone was sure to be along eventually. He just had to wait until that happened.

"Maybe," he thought to himself, "Amy will even ride out with her gun and come find me here."

He kept his hand on his dagger, feeling the warmth of the hilt against his palm and drawing slight comfort from his thought. As he sat there, waiting on the seconds to roll into minutes, he began to feel sleepy. Could he realistically stay awake until someone came, or until sunrise if no one did? As the minutes passed he became less certain that he could. What was the thing doing, anyway? He could feel the darkness pressing in on him. Looking at the moon he could see the red tint had reached a new level of darkness, covering almost the entire lunar surface and diminishing his ability to see around him. As the murky redness grew he began to feel like he was being watched. Somehow this wolf thing, or whatever it was, was out there in the darkness watching him, waiting on him to mess up somehow. If he got out the thing would be on him quickly, he felt sure, but what if he stayed? He could imagine the thing out in the darkness growing impatient as it watched him, smelled his fear, its hunger growing by the minute.

He knew if he fell asleep the thing would be on him in a second, coming in any way it could and taking his life as quickly as it had taken his car. But what if he didn't? What if he could actually stay awake and bide his time? Would the thing give up and go hunt something else? Could it really be that easy? He didn't think so. He could see it in his head, out in the darkness, watching him, growing more frustrated and hungry by the second. He could almost sense its hunger and anger, nearly driving it mad as it waited. Would it wait much longer? He didn't think so. He imagined what would happen if the thing attacked the car while he was in it. He would be trapped. He imagined it throwing itself at the windshield, covering him in a shower of glass before ripping him to shreds and picking his flesh from his bones. He shivered as he imagined every scenario he could, with only one seeming to hold promise. He would have to take a chance and run for it. At least if he got out of the car, he might have a chance at getting away. If he was attacked while sitting here on the side of the road, there would be little to no opportunity for him to even fight back, much less get away.

He felt there was only one option. He couldn't get his car out of the ditch from inside and he had a toolkit in his trunk. Maybe he could have a chance at fixing whatever was wrong with the front end if he looked, but he couldn't do it without making an effort. He slid his phone into his pocket and steeled himself for action. He threw the door open and popped the trunk, hopping out and running around, grabbing the toolkit and flashlight, listening to the night around him. He heard nothing. He ran to the front of the car, suddenly very aware of just how close he was to the thick brush at the edge of the field. Dropping to his knees he shined the flashlight under the car, hoping he would see the problem, and more than anything, hoping that it would be something he could solve. The light shone brightly, showing him that the tires were fine, both still attached, one not touching the ground. Looking farther he could see the axle was still in one piece. This led him to the problem, however. He had hit the creek bed at the exact wrong spot, his car finding the one thing that would prevent him from correcting his mistake. He had went over and gotten lodged on top of a small boulder that hadn't yet been worn down by the water. He cursed his luck, wishing death on whatever the animal was that had caused him to swerve and wreck in such a way.

He stood, replacing the tool kit in his trunk and grasping the handle of his dagger again, weighing his options. He watched the moon above as it turned almost completely red, only a thin sliver of the orb not covered in the Earth's shadow. He could climb back into the car and wait, like he had originally thought of doing, but now that he knew for sure there was no way to get his car out without help, he felt that was a worse option. But what other choice did he have? Walk? He had no idea exactly how far he had gone, or how much farther ahead his destination was. He knew Amy had said that he would be getting signal not long after reaching the forest because the road began to rise again, climbing out of the small valley, but he couldn't see such a thing ahead of him. All he could see in the growing darkness was the edge of the forest, tall and oppressing, threatening to swallow him whole if he got much closer. Beyond that he could see the swell of the mountains that surrounded the valley, but he had no way of knowing must how far out they were, nor could he tell which way the road went and how far he would have to try to go through that pitch darkness.

As he stood there leaning against the trunk of his car, the sound of movement picked up again from behind him, the sound of something creeping through the brush, louder than it would have been on a normal night. He didn't notice at first, but soon it registered and his fear grew again. He was now outside the car, his body totally exposed to whatever may want to attack him, and he couldn't tell where it was or how close it was getting. He turned his flashlight toward the sound, its thick beam cutting through the darkness slowly, illuminating a narrow cone of the night. He saw only brush and weeds waving slightly in the light breeze, making it impossible for him to tell exactly where the thing was. He began to back away, knowing now that there was no way could stand to sit in the car all night, just waiting to be attacked. He had to try to get away. As he made this decision the sound of movement grew louder, more deliberate, as if something wanted him to know it was coming. This solidified his decision and he turned, beginning to run toward the forest as fast as he could manage.

Expecting to hear a roar or a growl from behind him, followed by the sound of some huge beast chasing him with murder on its mind, he was surprised to only hear his own footsteps, his boots pounding the road like the gavel of a judge decreeing someone's guilt. He slowed down a bit, feeling that he should pace himself if he expected to actually make it a significant distance, soon slowing more until he was just taking a brisk walk. He knew if he walked it would take longer, but it would also allow him to conserve energy for the moment he would need it. He entered the forest with reluctance, the dying light of the now almost fully blood-red moon being too weak to pierce the veil of darkness in the woods. He used his flashlight to see as far ahead as possible, only allowing a small portion to touch the road in front of him, feeling he should be able to see as much of the darkness as possible, in case he did need to run again. To his right he thought he could still hear the soft sounds of movement, matching his own, but growing no closer to the road. Why would the animal be following him this long? Why prolong the attack, letting his fear and anxiety make him nearly crazy?

Tyler walked and walked, feeling his legs begin to get tired as he travelled the worn pavement, hoping for any sign of an incline to indicate that he might soon get cell service again. The sounds of sneaking from beside of him had ceased, he realized after he'd been walking for what felt like an hour. He stopped in his tracks, turning around once, shining the light as far as he could into the thick trees around him, hoping for a glimpse of whatever had been keeping up with him. He saw nothing. Could it be that it had given up on him and gone on to find something else to hunt? Could his entering the forest have been the thing that saved his life? He hoped so. He began to walk on at a slightly slower pace, his hand still wrapped tight around the handle of his dagger. He walked on farther, seeing what looked like a bit of light on the road ahead. He wasn't sure what it was, but felt certain it could be good for him. He walked on, a little cautious, his spine tingling as if he were still being watched, his brain telling him that he was more than likely still being followed.

As Tyler approached the light spot, he realized that it was a small clearing in the forest. Amy hadn't mentioned this. He stopped at the edge, letting his eyes adjust to the little light that remained from the almost completely covered moon that now sat right overhead, its murky, ominous red light bearing down on him like an evil eye in the sky. After another moment's hesitation, Tyler entered the clearing, immediately looking for a way out. A chill ran down his back as he stepped back into the deep red moonlight, his flashlight seeking the other side of the clearing ahead with no luck. He walked on the road, trying to speed up a bit, his hand trembling as a terrible feeling filled his heart. Sweat drenched his body as he became aware of every single movement around him. He was walking in near silence, not hearing the sound of anything following him when a twig snapped just off the edge of the road. He spun around, turning his flashlight to the darkness. As he scanned the edge of the road quickly, he caught two large points of light reflected back at him. It took him a moment to process what he'd seen, finally recognizing them as his light reflecting back at him from the retinas of an animal whose face looked to be on the same, if not a higher level than his own.

He moved his light back to the place he'd seen the eyes, now finding it empty. He had been so stupid, he realized now as he looked through the brush and into the forest. He couldn't hear the sound of the dead grass anymore because it had ended at the edge of the forest, smothered in layers of dead and rotting leaves. The perfect sound insulator. Of course the animal he was avoiding would be able to walk through the forest without making a sound. That was a predator's biggest advantage in this area most of the time. As he scanned the forest again, he moved sideways, trying to begin his escape again. Another twig snapped, this one coming from the place he'd been standing just a few moments before. Turning again, he faced the road he had just come up, terrified that he was making the hunt far too easy for whatever it was that had decided he would make a good meal. As a third twig snapped, this one from directly to his left, seeming so close he felt he could reach out and touch whatever caused it, a low growl began to sound through the small open space. Whatever was hunting him now knew he was aware of its proximity, he realized as he turned to his left, facing the forest head on. The growl grew louder as he peered into the darkness, trying to see whatever was there. A fourth twig snap told him his answer was just feet away, making his heart jump into overtime.

As he made this realization he couldn't take it anymore. He broke out and ran the way he had been going, trying desperately to reach the incline that would take him out of the forest and give him the only chance of salvation he could think of. He heard a roar from behind him as his would-be attacker crashed through the underbrush, chasing him from the forest, thrashing plants and weeds in order to attempt to overtake him again. His heart slammed against his ribs as the thrashing noises drew up and sounded right beside of him, making him dreadfully aware that whatever was chasing him could leap from the forest at him at any second. Pushing himself harder than ever, he kept going, attempting to squash his fear and beat the beast in the forest that wanted to make him its next meal. He ran with all of his might, his breath ragged and hot against his dry throat. His legs screamed in weariness and pain as he pushed them harder than he ever had before. The edge of the clearing was ahead, he realized as he looked up, the sound of thrashing and growling now accompanied by the wheezing breath of the animal in the forest.

Tyler could hear each inhalation, followed by a growling, wet sounding exhalation that made his blood run cold. The beast kept pace with him for a few seconds, making him nervous, but soon the sound changed positions, making his heart soar for just a moment. The sound continued to change, but now the underbrush was also moving in the light of his flashlight. The creature that was after him hadn't fallen behind, it had drawn ahead to cut him off. As this thought registered in his mind a large shadow burst forth from the foliage, making him skid to a stop, falling backwards on the road, his flashlight still pointing forward. The sound of growling rose to an all new level as the animal picked itself up from the road. Tyler was frozen in place as he watched the wheezing beast unfold itself to stand on all fours and face him. Deep, glowing red eyes locked onto him as his light illuminated them again. As he witnessed the beast he recognized it perfectly.

It bared its long yellow fangs, allowing saliva to run freely down its jowls and drip on the road in thick, white ropes. Dark black fur covered the body of the larger than average wolf, the long hind legs ending in thick canine paws, while the front legs ended in a bastardized cross between hands and paws. As he stared at the creature it tensed its back legs and straightened its back, rising onto its hind legs, its arms bulging as it closed its paw like hands into fists, making it rise to a height of more than 7 feet tall. They stood there staring at each other, neither moving for a few moments. Tyler looked up into the beast's eyes and saw a hatred unlike anything he had ever imagined. He'd dreamed of the beast, but seeing it in real life, feeling its hate, its hot, wet breath blowing over him from the short distance, made him truly fear for his life in a way he never had. The wolf growled a deep, menacing growl that, to Tyler, almost sounded as if it was trying to say his name. His breath caught in his chest as he realized this was the moment he had been waiting for. The beast that had haunted his every thought for the last week was standing in front of him, larger than life, and he couldn't even make himself move.

As if sensing this thought, the wolf hunched over, putting itself in a position that would let it pounce on him with little to no effort. The wolf's movement broke his hesitation, freeing him to attempt to defend himself. He crouched low to the ground, spreading his legs a bit and squaring his shoulders, drawing his dagger from its sheath and keeping his light trained on the wolf so he would know its every movement. The wolf looked at his blade and snarled loudly as if it knew what the weapon was intended to do. It opened its fists, brandishing its claws as it opened its jaws wide, saliva dripping from the jagged fangs that Tyler knew could easily tear him to shreds and make him very easy to digest. Tyler knew the wolf was going to move before it actually did. The wolf leaped forward, snapping its jaws closed where Tyler's shoulder had been just a second before as he rolled away and brought himself back up on one knee, shining his light in the angry wolf's face. So many emotions filled Tyler's head at once, but the ones that influenced his actions the most were a combination of confusion at what this thing was and anger that it was keeping him from Amy.

The image of Amy filled his head for a split second, not Amy as he remembered her from the last few days, but of the torn and bleeding Amy from the nightmare he'd had. The creature in front of him configured its face in what Tyler would have sworn was an evil attempt at a smile and struck again. This time it reached out for him rather than attempting to bite him, the claws on its right hand slashing across his back as he spin away, opening the skin easily. He felt fresh, hot blood pouring down his back as the warm night air started it drying almost instantly. He winced as the searing pain became worse, sweat running down his back and into the fresh wounds. The wolf brought its paw to its snout, sniffing lightly before touching one claw to its tongue. Tyler could see his blood on the monster's tongue for a split second before it closed its mouth and swallowed. A shiver went through the creature's body, its eyes shooting open. It dropped to a crouch and turned its head back to the sky, letting out a howl that nearly deafened Tyler. Risking a glance upwards, Tyler could see that the moon was completely red now, a bloody hole in the sky the only sign the satellite even existed.

The wolf wasted no time in its third attack. As Tyler was bringing his head back down, it pounced, huge front paws landing on his chest, long fingers wrapping around his shoulders, the claws digging into his skin. He went down quickly, the breath rushing out of his body as the weight of the wolf forced him to remain on the ground. It sat on his pelvis, its body so long that the end of its tail curled around the bottom of his left foot, while it had to hunch its back to look down into his eyes. Hot, sticky saliva dripped off its fangs, splattering on his face and chest, making his skin tingle and crawl where it landed on him. He tried to sit up and throw the wolf off of him, but it was just too heavy. He could move his legs just a little, but that only made the wolf reposition itself whenever he managed to move his legs enough to even slightly dislodge it from its current position. It bent its face down to his, snout less than an inch from his skin and began to sniff him, starting at his hairline and not ending until it reached his chest. He found himself whining ever so slightly in his fear and anger, the monster hovering over him paying the sound no mind. It darted its tongue out once, licking the flesh of his right cheek and making his skin crawl, drawing a sound of indignation from him. It closed its eyes, as if relishing the taste of him. He was determined not to let it get another.

His shoulders were pinned, so he knew he wouldn't have much range with it, but he realized that he had managed to hold onto his knife in the fall. Bracing himself as the wolf opened its mouth again, he jammed the knife into its side as best he could. He felt the blade scrape against the wolf's ribs, and imagined it slicing open at least one or two major organs. He twisted the blade and jerked it back out as the wolf pulled away from the source of its pain, a scream that sounded terrifyingly human escaping its throat before being replaced by a growl that undoubtedly held malicious intent.

Tyler took his chance and pushed the wolf off of him, leaping away and keeping his light trained on the creature, watching as blood ran down its side. It stared him in the eyes, daring him to turn away or even so much as blink. He backed slowly down the road, putting as much distance between him and the now injured wolf as possible. The wounded creature slowly stood back up, stretching its abdomen and reopening the wound that had begun to stop bleeding. Fresh blood poured out of the wolf's side as it reared back its head and roared again, this time sounding angry and vengeful. It looked Tyler in the eyes and snarled at him, bracing its legs before leaping at him again.

Tyler leaped to the side as the creature bounded forward, pushing itself with its front paws as it fell short of him. He swung his blade hard as the wolf ran by him, unable to adjust as quickly as he could. He felt the knife make contact and heard another of those inhuman screams. The wolf tumbled to the ground, rubbing its face against the gravel as if it had an itch. When it turned to him and stood he saw that he'd cut its face. In just an instant the wound had turned an ugly red, swelling out from its face as if he had branded the wolf with a hot poker. A quick glance told him that the wound on its side had done the same thing. He looked at the dagger in his hand, seeing its blade still remarkably free of blood despite the fountains pouring from the wolf. The wound in its face had added to the nest of scars that covered the small portions of exposed skin, fresh blood running down its face, soaking and matting the hair on its chest. It bared its teeth again, the skin of its face now hanging down in a flap that exposed the entire left side of its mouth, blood and saliva running down over the swollen flesh. It lunged a third time, from only a yard away.

Tyler had nowhere to go. Thinking on his feet, he did the only thing that seemed possible. He lunged forward as well. Diving at the thing's feet, he rolled and shoved his dagger upward, catching the wolf in the thigh and bringing it down on top of him. Its weight pinned him again as he struggled to remove his blade, the howling of the pained animal making him cringe in agony. He thrashed his legs as the beast's claws dug into his back, cleaving flesh from bone as the wolf paid him back for his attacks. He kicked at the wolf as hard as he could, relishing in glory when he felt his foot make contact. He tried to move his hands to allow him to stab the thing again, knowing that he was closer to beating it than he ever thought possible. He pushed the dagger with all his might, feeling it sink into the soft flesh of the wolf's stomach at the same time he felt the thing's huge jaws close around his leg.

He screamed in pain, trying to tug his leg from the jaws of the beast, feeling his flesh rip as the fangs sank in so deep they scratched his bone. He twisted the blade in his hand, pushing harder, feeling the wolf's guts turn to mush beneath the force of the blade. Finally the thing released his leg, bellowing a scream of pain that matched his own, rolling off of him in order to free itself of the pain of the blade that now seemed to be hot to the touch, even to Tyler. He pulled himself away from the wolf, feeling his body begin to go into shock from the pain and blood loss. He knew he had to keep himself awake. He used all of the effort he could muster and forced himself to sit up, finding his flashlight and shining the light on his leg. He could move it above the knee, but the wolf's bite had shredded almost every inch of flesh and muscle from his knee to his ankle.

Tyler gritted his teeth against the pain and shined his light upward, searching for his attacker. He saw the wolf lying in the road a little farther up from him, looking somehow smaller than it had. He saw the moon above him begin to reemerge on the other side of the red shadow, a white beacon in the murky darkness. The thing in the road looked up at him, its eyes no longer glowing red and tried to make a sound. The light of the moon seemed to comfort it as it looked up into the sky. As he watched the beast became obscured by a mist that seemed to raise from its body, its face bubbling as if changing. The wound on its cheek closed, as did the one he could see on its leg, and its mouth seemed to retract into its face. He felt himself begin to slide out of consciousness as he tried to crawl up the road to get away from the beast that had done this. The world around him grew black, despite the light in his hand. The last thing he saw before the darkness took over was the flesh of his leg knitting itself back together as the beast in the road looked at him, the face obscured by the mist that rose from its body seeming remarkably human and eerily familiar.

***

Tyler awoke slowly to the sound of a fan blowing pleasantly cool air onto his face, birds chirping somewhere in the background. He was aware that he was in a soft bed, just as he was aware that he wasn't wearing any clothes. Neither of these things bothered him as he lay there, keeping his eyes closed to block out the light of the day. It felt just like any other day waking up in his own soft bed, he thought as he stretched - except his bed didn't have a headboard. And come to think of it, he didn't have a fan like the one he felt on his face. He opened his eyes slowly, the light of the day instantly making him shut them again and cringe against the unfamiliar pillow.

"Tyler," he heard a lovely voice say from nearby. "Kayla, he's waking up."

"Thank God," came another familiar voice from outside of the room.

"Amy," he said, his voice coming out a sharp, low rasp against his painfully dry throat. "Water. Please."

"Of course," she said, her hand instantly on his head, guiding his mouth toward a glass of water so cool it practically cut his tongue. He slurped it all down in seconds and asked for a second and a third.

"What happened," he said, clearing his throat now that his thirst was finally partially quenched.

"We were hoping you could tell us."

"What do you mean," he said, opening his eyes again, forcing them to stay open this time.

"We found you in the middle of the road, naked, beside your car."

"Seriously?"

"Yeah," Kayla said, looking at his bare chest as he sat up. "It wasn't a bad sight, either," she teased. "Amy's a lucky girl."

"Kayla," Amy said, her blush crawling up from her neck in the way Tyler loved.

He struggled to remember what had happened before he woke up in the bed and came up mostly blank. He remembered going home to check on the dog and getting pinned.

"Buddy," he said.

"What about him?"

"He pinned me," Tyler said, struggling to remember, getting only recollections of pain, the image of his shredded leg playing through his mind's eye. "I think he attacked me. My leg," he said, pulling the covers off his lower body to find his leg intact.

"Honey, your leg is fine," Amy said, pulling the sheets back over his crotch and laying her hand on his thigh. "Do you really not remember?"

"I don't know. I remember going home. He pinned me and then..." he closed his eyes and relaxed, trying to remember what had happened. He knew he had left his house with a knife after putting the dog inside and then he drew a blank. "Did I have a dagger?"

"Yeah," Amy said, pulling the long weapon out of the floor under the bed. "This was on the passenger seat of your car with your wallet, phone and flashlight."

He took the dagger in his hands, trying to remember the night. He unsheathed the blade slowly, looking for anything to jar his memory. There were no markings on the blade at all. He felt his hand growing hot as he held the hilt. Slowly he touched his finger to the blade and jerked his hand back, feeling as though he'd touched the edge of a hot pan. He felt the pain from the blade enter his body, and was frozen as his memories came rushing back, making him rigid with fear.

"Where is it," he yelled, the blade now firm in his hand.

"Where is what," Amy asked, jumping away as if terrified he meant to stab her.

"The wolf," he said, sheathing the blade and laying it back under the bed. "The wolf. It attacked me. I killed it. Or...I think I did."

"Honey, what are you talking about?"

Tyler asked to speak with Amy alone, Kayla obliging after telling him she was glad he was OK. Once she had left them in private and closed the door he turned to Amy and recounted his entire night to her. Once he had finished by telling her of seeing his father's face grow from that of the wolf she looked at him dumbfounded.

"Sweetie," she said slowly. "Like I said, we found you by your car."

"Naked. With my knife, phone and wallet in the car."

"Yes."

"And how do you think that happened?"

"Well, we don't know. I thought maybe someone stole your clothes and left everything else."

"Amy, honey, who is going to steal my clothes and then leave my rare knife, wallet and smartphone in my car?"

"I don't know. Someone who just needed clothes?"

"No, dear. That doesn't happen. I can show you where it happened. How did you find me?"

"We realized it had been three hours since we'd heard from you and I got terrified. We got our guns and drove out looking. We saw your car as soon as we left the woods. We..."

"You what?"

"We almost didn't see you. Neither of us was expecting you to be IN the road. I spotted you at the last second and Kayla slammed on the brakes."

"How long did it take you to clean me up?"

"What do you mean?"

"I'll admit my wounds obviously weren't as bad as I thought, but I know I was hurt. I don't look a bit bloody and I don't see a single scar. As a matter of fact, I feel better than I have in a while."

"Honey, there was nothing wrong with you. You were just out. You were naked as the day you were born and sleeping like a rock. There wasn't a mark on you. We got you in the truck and got your things. I wanted to take you to a hospital, but Kayla said we should tend to you ourselves first."

"That's impossible, Amy. I remember the wolf scratching and biting me. I can still feel its claws and teeth in my skin. I know it tore me to shreds."

"I don't know, honey. Maybe someone hit you over the head and you had another one of your nightmares."

"No. I know that wasn't it. It can't have been. This one was too real. I can still see it, feel its breath. This happened, Amy."

"Tyler, I don't know what to tell you. I really don't. If you think something that serious happened we can take you to a doctor and have you checked out."

"No, I don't think that's going to help. Something weird is happening here. I just need to rest. If you think I'm fine, then I guess I'm fine."

"Are you sure? Maybe you should have someone look…"

"Look at what?"

"Well, your head… "

"So you think I'm nuts?"

"No honey, but you're saying your leg was ruined and your back was in tatters, and we never saw a mark on you. We looked for injuries and didn't find any."

"Did you check my head?"

Amy remained silent, looking at the floor as if ashamed.

"Did you?"

"Yes."

"And did you find anything?"

"No. But-"

"Honey, I'm not trying to fight. I can't thank you enough for taking care of me. I just know something happened to me out there and I can't figure out what's going on. How long was I asleep?"

"Well, we found you a little after three and it's almost noon now so not all that long. At least around nine hours. Maybe ten depending on what happened."

"Ten hours and everything seems so different."

"What do you mean?"

"Well, I just don't feel scared. Does that make sense? I just had some kind of...I don't know what...where I watched and felt this wolf thing rip me a new one, but I feel fine. Better than fine."

"Maybe it's because you finally fought back again."

"Well, in the second dream I killed it, remember."

"Yeah. I don't know. Maybe this one just gave you the right closure?"

"I guess. I don't know. I'm sorry I never made it back. I tried hard."

"I know. You're OK."

"I'm not much of a protector if I can't even drive to you right."

"Honey, you're fine. We made it through the night and everything is fine. I think I've even talked Kayla into staying."

"How did you manage that?"

"We just talked a lot about Doug. She still has reservations about her dog, but I think she wants to stay."

"Did you ever see anything else last night?"

"No. I heard some movement in the bushes as we were leaving to look for you, but out here that could have been anything."

"Good. I hope Buddy's OK in the house. I think we should go check on him soon."

"We will. I want you to eat first, though. Kayla said she was going to cook whenever you woke up."

"She already is," he said, turning his nose up. "Bacon." His stomach growled loudly enough to startle both of them as he smelled the food, making him laugh and throw the sheets off of him. "Let's go help," he said walking towards the door.

"Hold on there, mister," she said, grabbing his hand and turning him around, grasping his crotch with the other hand. "Forgetting something?"

"Good point. But I'm not sure what I'm supposed to do about it. My clothes are gone."

"Kayla found some things you can try, if you want to."

He looked at the pile of clothes she referred to, picking out an old pair of bicycle shorts from the pile and sliding them on.

"They're tight enough to take my pulse in, but it's the only thing here that's good. Besides, you've both already seen me naked. You a few times," he said, winking at her as he turned for the door again, pausing before he opened it and turning around.

"Yes," Amy said, looking at him with a grin.

"I'm glad you're OK. And I can't thank you enough," he said, wrapping her in a tight embrace, kissing her lips passionately before looking her in the eyes, finally unafraid of saying the words he'd avoided. "I love you, Amy."

"I love you, too, Tyler," she said, meaning it.

"One of the things that kept me going last night was the thought of getting to you. I was terrified I'd never see you again, never get to tell you that. I do. I love you."

"I love you, too," she said, still taken aback by the fact that he said it first.

"I'm glad to hear you say that," he said, kissing her softly before guiding her to the door and letting her lead him through the unfamiliar house.

They chatted with Kayla while they helped her cook, all of them attempting to avoid the subject of the previous night. When the food was ready Tyler was unable to help himself as he filled his plate with a mountain of food. He ate more than he normally would and still his stomach wanted more. He topped his food off with two huge glasses of water in the hopes that they would help settle his hunger until he was in a place he wouldn't be so ashamed of stuffing his face. They talked for a while longer, Tyler thanking Kayla again for helping to find him and giving him a place to sleep off whatever had happened to him, not willing to talk about his night again. He was still certain it hadn't been a dream, but had no idea how to prove it. Soon enough, he and Amy both voiced that they should go check on the dog and get his car moved, Tyler making a slight offhand comment about changing his clothes, as well, smiling as the two women laughed pleasantly. Tyler gathered the belongings they'd brought from his car, checking his phone and finding it nearly dead. He held the knife by the sheath, the hilt still making his hand uncomfortably hot for some reason.

"What did you do with the dog," Tyler asked as they walked down the steps, giving the blood stain a few feet of clearance.

"Um...Nothing," Amy said, peering back at the house uncomfortably.

"Well, he's not here, now. Are you sure Kayla didn't move him?"

"It's possible. I stayed in the room with you from the time we brought you until you woke up. But she didn't mention it to me."

"Should we ask?"

"I think it would be best if we didn't."

Tyler crouched for a second, looking for signs of where the dog's body might have gone and finding a short, bloody track of matted grass to one side. He elected not to mention this to Amy, after seeing the look on her face.

"Besides," he thought, "she already thinks I'm crazy. Why give her more fuel?"

But what if she was right? Something very strange had happened last night, no matter how you looked at it. Tyler's present state was very different than how he should be, based on his memory of the things that occurred after his wreck. He should be hospitalized at least, if not dead from shock and blood loss. He climbed into the car beside Amy, resting his head against her leather headrest.

"How far from the house was I," he asked as she backed down the driveway.

"Not far. You'll see. You were a little over halfway through the dead zone, actually."

"That figures."

They rode in silence down the back road, both of them making an effort to enjoy the scenery in silence, letting each other rest after the excitement of the night before. As they descended the mountain, Tyler began to grow a bit uneasy, his stomach suddenly churning as if wanting to reject the food he'd eaten. As the road levelled out, the trees thinned, bringing them into a small clearing. Tyler recognized it instantly, his eyes scanning the road for what he felt certain would be there.

"Stop," he shouted suddenly. "Amy, stop!"

"What is it, honey," she asked, slamming on the brakes.

Tyler leaped out of the car and ran to the spot he'd seen, the spot he'd known would be there. He crouched down, touching it and finding it dry. Amy followed him out of the car, questioning him, her fear so strong he thought he could smell it.

"Right here," he said, pointing to the large blood stain on the road. "I told you. This is the stain."

"Tyler, honey, animals get hit on this road all of the time. That could be any kind of blood."

"No, Amy, I'm telling you," he said, walking back to where he figured he had been lying and seeing a smaller blood stain that he guessed had come from his back. "This is where I was, where I rolled on my back and passed out. I watched it bleed here."

"Tyler, please. Let's just get in the car."

"I need you to move the car a little."

"Tyler..."

"Please, Amy."

She obliged, driving her car down past the first blood stain he had pointed out and running back to him as he crouched in the road over another stain, bracing himself with his hand. As she approached he lifted the hand and looked at her slowly.

"Now you have to believe me," he said, gesturing to the mark in the road that was undoubtedly a bloody handprint made by something with the most grotesque humanoid claws she'd ever imagined.

***

"I still don't understand," Amy said for the third time.

"Everything I told you was true," he said, almost as shocked as she was after showing her the spot where he had been bitten, his own boot prints clear even on the dirty road, the blood from where he'd attempted to gut the wolf a darker and thicker color than the rest.

"But how? You're fine. There literally isn't a scratch on you. We checked."

"I believe you. I feel almost no pain. I don't understand how that's possible. My back was shredded to bits. I could tell. But the only thing that hurts is the bone of my leg, I guess where its teeth scraped."

"This isn't possible. Please tell me this is some joke."

"I wish it was."

"Tyler Randolph, if I find out you're pulling some prank on me…"

"Amy, honey, if I was playing a joke, I promise you it would not involve killing a dog. What kind of man do you think I am?"

"You're right. I'm sorry. I just. I don't know. I'm so confused."

"When you got my stuff out of the car, did you check to see if I had been robbed?"

"No, actually. We figured since they left the knife and the phone that they wouldn't take the money."

He pulled the wallet out of the bag Kayla had given him for his few belongings and opened it, expecting it to be empty. What he found shocked him more than he could describe. Every bit of money he'd had was in the wallet, his debit card was in its slot as well. The real shock came from what was staring back at him out of the clear compartment designed to house his I.D. He looked at Amy, looking back at his wallet and blinking, sliding his finger in the compartment to touch the paper and make sure it was real. Looking back at him from where his driver's license was housed was a note written in a substance that he was positive was blood. The note consisted of three words and read, simply;

it was real.

***

Once they'd arrived at his house, giving him time to shower and dress as Amy checked on the dog, they called a tow truck to haul his car from its resting place, asking them to just bring it to his house so he could fix it. They made themselves a nice lunch of steak and fries, Tyler eating two large steaks rare enough they looked able to get up and walk off of the plate, soaking up the remaining blood and juices with his fries, while Amy nursed her own small steak for a long time.

"Tyler," she said, as he was finishing his food, "what do we do?"

"What do you mean," he said, realizing he hadn't even considered the question he was sure she was asking him.

"About you. Should we take you to a doctor?"

"Why?"

"You say you were viciously attacked, and you showed me the stains. I'm not a doctor, but based on what you told me and the amount of blood that was in the road, I'm not sure how you're alive."

"I feel fine," he said, feeling a little angry that she still couldn't accept what he'd told her.

"I know, but how? And what happened to your clothes? And what happened to the wolf?"

"I don't know, Amy," he said, a little more forcefully than he intended, feeling a strange anger welling up within himself. "I have no idea what the hell is going on, but I really don't think a doctor is going to be much help at this point," he said, forcing himself to calm down.

"I just don't want you to be sick and us not know it."

"I know. I don't think I am."

"OK. But promise me that if you start to feel strange, or if anything else happens, you'll tell me and let me take care of you."

"I promise," he said. "Where's Buddy?"

"He wanted back outside."

"Let's go sit with him. If I stay in here around the food I'm going to keep eating. You don't want a fat boyfriend, do you?"

They laughed as they walked to the porch, Amy making a mental note of his appetite for the second time that day. Tyler opened the screen door and was instantly shocked by the state of the dog who had taken so kindly to him of late. Buddy was standing on the bench by the door, the hair on his back bristled up, a confused look in his eyes. He began growling, low and deep in his throat as Tyler stepped out so Amy could come outside.

"Buddy," Tyler said, holding his hand out so the dog could smell him, "what's wrong you silly dog?"

"Be careful. Don't let him bite you."

"He won't," Tyler said, moving closer to the dog who was now whining and looking torn. "Will you boy?"

Once Tyler was close, Buddy turned his head and sniffed the man's hand, giving it a lick once he determined his new friend wasn't a threat and sitting down, looking around as if he was uneasy.

"Did something spook you, boy," Tyler asked, walking up and petting the dog until his tail began to wag.

"He was fine when I let him out."

"Maybe he just thought I was going to make him go back inside. I think he's happier out here."

"That could be it," Amy said, not knowing whether or not she believed it.

They played with the dog for a bit, Tyler running around the yard and rolling around with him in a way she'd never seen. She began to think that he was being fully honest, and he really did feel better than ever. She had no idea what had happened on that road, but she'd heard his version of the story, and she'd seen the blood in the road. Those things alone were enough to make her think that maybe the dreams he'd been having had somehow had some basis in reality. One thing she was certain of as she watched this man who suddenly looked more muscular than he had in the few months she'd known him, is that she may have no idea just what she'd gotten herself into.

***

Tyler's behavior remained much the same for the next couple of days. He found that he was often hungry, he typically craved meat and usually preferred it rare, which wasn't a change from his normal routine, but he found that he wanted larger portions and wanted it more often. He tried his best to keep these things from Amy, eating as much as he could handle whenever he ate a meal on his own, but he could tell she was still wary. Their love life was helped a lot by the fact that the police were unable to allow them to reopen the tour center. Their celebration was hindered a bit on the Monday after Tyler was attacked when Amy got a call from Kayla, who had news none of them expected to receive.

"What's wrong," Tyler asked Amy once she hung up, noticing the look on her face as she joined him on the couch.

"Doug."

"What about him, honey?"

"He's gone."

"Amy," Tyler said, leaning up to put his arm around her. "Doug was killed five days ago."

"I know. I mean, he's gone. His body is gone from the morgue. The police were going to do the autopsy tomorrow and his body is nowhere to be found."

"Could he have been buried in someone else's place," Tyler said, somehow knowing that wasn't the case.

"They don't seem to think so. Apparently no one has checked on him in three days, so they actually have no idea when he disappeared."

"Oh wow. How's Kayla taking it?"

"She's furious and hurt. She trusted them to take care of him and they did this. She feels like something is terribly wrong. Of course, she brought up Sunday."

"What about Sunday?"

"She said something about her dog, and said maybe it really was Doug. I couldn't really understand her at that point. She was mumbling. I think she was a little drunk."

"In the middle of the day?"

"Well, the man she loved was killed, honey. I'd probably be drunk myself if…"

"If what?"

"Well, if you hadn't been alive when we found you."

"Don't think like that," he said, squeezing her tight. "I'm fine."

"Are you," she asked him slowly.

"Of course. Why wouldn't I be?"

"I don't know. I'm just so confused by everything that's been happening."

"So am I. You can talk to me, you know."

"I know. I just don't want to upset you."

"You won't. I'm here for you. We have to be able to talk about anything."

"I just noticed you eating more and other things. Maybe it's not unusual. I mean, we haven't been together all that long. Maybe I just never noticed it before."

"I guess I've been eating a little more. I don't know. I think I just have more of an appetite right now."

"But why?"

"Well, I'm happier. I don't have as much stress. I've got you, we're on a sort of vacation, I've not been having the dreams. Things are looking up a bit."

"You haven't had any nightmares?"

"Not that I can recall. Not since Saturday."

"You've thrashed in your sleep for a couple of nights now. I think I even heard you moaning one night."

"Oh. I don't know. I don't remember them and I haven't woken up screaming, so they can't be that bad. I'm telling you, Amy. I'm great. I feel like a million bucks."

"OK. Do you think you're OK on your own for a night?"

"If I have to be, but do you not want to stay?"

"I want to, honey, believe me," she said, kissing him deeply. "But Kayla is pretty out of shape. I don't want her to...you know..."

"I understand. No way she could come here?"

"I don't think it would help. I think she needs a girl's night."

"OK. If she needs you don't worry about anything here. I'll make do with goofball out there. Maybe we'll hunt down some deer and eat from nature tonight," he said, flashing his teeth at her jokingly.

"I'm not sure calling him goofball is giving yourself justice," she said, ruffling his hair before kissing his stubbly cheek. "Are you trying to grow your beard out?"

"Not really," he said, rubbing his face. "I shaved this morning, remember?"

"I thought you had. Maybe it's time to change razors."

"Don't you like me with a little more scruff?"

"It looks good, but it itches me to death," she said, scratching her face.

"I'll see what I can do," he said, grabbing her and rubbing his chin across her cheek before kissing her tenderly.

They spent a few more minutes together before Amy gathered a few of her belongings and they walked to their cars together.

"Are you going somewhere," Amy asked as he locked the door behind him.

"Yeah, I'm running to the store. If I'm playing the bachelor again tonight I'm going to need some chips and junk food," he said, knowing that his only real concern was meat, and a lot of it.

"Sounds absolutely primitive," she laughed, flipping her hair over her shoulder as she unlocked her car, smiling when he opened the door for her. "You know, you keep that up and someone might think you're a gentleman."

"Then I'll impolitely belch right in their face," he said, kissing her once before closing her door and walking around his own recently fixed car.

"Are you sure that thing is good to go?"

"Of course. I fixed it myself," he said, puffing out his chest and acting offended. "Why wouldn't it work perfectly?"

"Well, you said it yourself; you're no mechanic."

He had jacked the car up and checked the undercarriage after realizing that it would still start just fine. He found a few torn hoses and refilled his spilled brake fluid, seeing that those seemed to be the only problems to find. "I'm sure it's fine, honey. I'll take it slow on the way out just in case. Text me when you get signal if you're worried."

"You know I will. I'll probably be texting you most of the night. I don't think she'll last much longer."

"Is she that much of a lightweight?"

"The last time we talked about drinking she told me she usually couldn't take more than 3 beers. She told me once I turn 21 she'd split a 6 pack with me and we'd see how it went."

"Sounds like a plan to me. Tell her I want in on that. I turn 21 before you do," he said laughing. "Just take care of her and keep her in the house."

"I'll try. You and Buddy be good and safe, OK?"

"Of course. And Amy," he started, hesitating as she looked his way again. "Stay in the house once you get there, OK? Keep your gun handy, too."

"After the other night I wouldn't do anything less. I love you," she said with a grin.

"I love you, too. I'll see you tomorrow?"

"As soon as possible."

Tyler got in his car, waving to Amy as she pulled away and drove into town, testing his new brake line out as he rounded the curves. His trip to the store was a quick one, his mind mercifully blank as he let the rock music soothe him while he navigated the road. Once he arrived at the store he went straight to the meat coolers, picking out a package of ground beef that weighed in at a little under 5 pounds. His stomach growled as he looked at the meat, making him feel like he could tear the package open and dig into it right there. He walked to the snack aisle and picked out some junk food and chips as well, knowing he needed to fill his stomach with more than just meat. As he was walking back to the front of the store a young man looking at his phone and not paying any attention to his surroundings rushed out of an aisle, hitting Tyler with his buggy hard enough to knock him into the deli container that held fresh chicken and ribs.

The heating lamps in the stand kept the metal at a scorching temperature, causing more people burns and blisters than the store cared to admit. Tyler was forced to brace himself against this metal for almost a half a minute in order to regain his footing and untangle himself from the cart that had hit him. The man behind the cart looked up, horrified to realize what he had done. By the time Tyler managed to free his arm from the display case, the smell of burning meat was prominent in the air. His arm was a road map of blisters, many of which burst the second he flexed the muscles in his arm. Tyler felt a fury unlike anything he'd ever experienced flow through his body. Without hesitating he grabbed the cart and began shouting at the man wielding it.

"What the hell do you think you're doing," he shouted, brushing off the hands around him that offered to get him help for his injury. "Why don't you watch where you're going instead of having your nose in that damn phone, jerk?"

The man stuttered an apology, unable to look at anything but Tyler's arm.

"What if it had been a little kid here instead of me? What if their face had slammed into that damn thing? How would you feel then you freaking moron," he said, his voice lowering to a growl as the anger took over. Without giving the man another chance for response, Tyler shoved the buggy in his hand backward into the man, sending both of them careening down the aisle as the handle knocked the wind out of the man.

He didn't bother waiting to see what happened next, pushing through the crowd and finding a register, checking out and getting to his car before anyone else had a chance to say anything to him, or worse make him angry again. He slammed his car door loudly, suddenly wondering why he'd gotten so angry. He didn't remember ever feeling anything like that in his life. As much as he hated to admit it to himself, he kind of liked letting the anger out like that. He knew it was overall very unproductive in a public setting, but for the moment it had worked. He raised his arm to look at the wound, hoping it was nothing he would need to see a doctor about and found himself looking at smooth skin. He had felt the blisters rise and burst on his arm, he was sure, but looking at it now there was nothing wrong with it, save the fact that it was very red. He touched it, wincing a little as he brushed the tender skin. He forced himself to lay his hand on it after this, realizing that his skin felt nearly as hot as the metal display had.

"I guess that makes sense," he said to the empty car. "I was on it for a good while so of course my skin is going to be hot."

But he was still uneasy. He was certain that there should be more than just hot, red skin after touching something that hot for so long. He had seen other customers walk away with blisters after just brushing the metal while getting something from inside of it, had actually had it happen to him once before. So how could he not be badly burnt right now? He drove out of the parking lot, not seeing anyone who had been witness to his retaliation against the idiot who had knocked him down. He tore into a bag of chips as he drove, eating a few at a time until he made his way out of the traffic and into the mountains, turning his attention back to the road and his music as he barreled up the curvy road, wanting to get home and eat quickly.

His mind wandered over the events of the last few days again as his stomach growled. He had eaten more in the last two days than he remembered eating in the entire week before his night on the road. He had begun referring to it as such because he couldn't honestly say that he had been attacked as he had no proof of such. His memory told him he should be bedridden or six feet under the ground, yet here he was, living and breathing and driving with the leg that, only three days ago, he had felt get shredded from knee to ankle.

His driveway popped into view before he knew it, causing him to really test his brakes as he whipped his car to the left and slid into his spot, grabbing the phone that he'd heard go off while he was driving. Amy had told him she was at Kayla's while he was wandering around in the store, sending another message just a few moments ago when she hadn't heard back from. He debated on telling her what had happened at the store but decided against, knowing she was already more worried about him than she cared to admit. He had seen her taking peeks at him, studying his face, his movements, when she though he wasn't looking. He told her he was fine, that he had been driving and asked how Kayla was.

He gathered his groceries and went up to the house, smiling when his phone went off right away. He could tell Amy had been worrying about him, as a matter of fact, she hadn't stopped since the other night. He unlocked his door and walked in only to be stopped in his tracks by the sound of growling. He turned to the left and saw the shadow of Buddy standing between the living room and the kitchen, his body tense and ready to pounce. He felt both offended and angry that the dog whose life he felt he had saved would act this way towards him when he needed the animal most.

"Buddy, what are you doing, crazy," he said, walking closer to the dog.

The growling stopped as the dog heard his voice, his tail wagging slightly back and forth. He approached the animal slowly, unsure what the issue was, but knowing he didn't want to spook the dog. Buddy raised his head, sniffing the air, whining a bit as his tail wagged faster.

"What's wrong, boy?"

Buddy backed up slowly as Tyler got closer, each step more hesitant than the last until Tyler stopped and reached his hand out, waiting on the dog to come to him. Buddy took one tentative step after the other, sniffing the air as he came, his tail twitching as if he was unsure whether he should wag it or not. Once the dog was close, it stretched its neck and sniffed his hand, licking it as he recognized Tyler's scent. His body remained tense and rigid as Tyler patted his head.

"What's going on, Buddy," he said, kneeling before his new friend, feeling saddened that the dog acted like he didn't know him anymore. Buddy approached him slowly, touching his warm, wet nose to Tyler's before licking his neck and nuzzling his face. Tyler patted his side and rubbed his shoulders until he seemed to relax a bit. As Tyler stood the dog jumped a little, crossing to his right side and sniffing at the arm Tyler had hurt before shaking his head, baring his teeth once before walking away as if he wanted nothing to do with the man. Tyler shook his own head slowly, not understanding the strange behavior the dog was exhibiting. He turned on a light in the kitchen and emptied his bag, going to the stove and getting a pan ready to cook his dinner. He tore into the package of meat and got a huge fistful, making it into a patty that looked big enough to cover a small plate, much less a bun. He did the same thing again, finding that he had used barely half of the package. He knew he would be hungry later, but the smell of the meat was intoxicating. He tossed a pinch of meat to Buddy, watching as the dog lapped it up with no hesitation.

He turned back to the stove, seasoning his burgers as they started to cook and saw the hunk of raw meat again, this time bending close to catch the smell. His stomach practically roared in approval of the food. Before he thought about it he grabbed a pinch between his fingers and placed it on his tongue, feeling the cool, soft texture squish between his teeth as he chewed. The sensation gave him a feeling of inexplicable satisfaction. He placed another pinch in his mouth and was bringing a third to his lips when the realization of what he was doing hit him.

Was he seriously standing here eating raw meat? People had been known to die just from having meat that was slightly undercooked and he was sitting here putting completely raw meat into his system. What the hell was going on with him? He wrapped the rest of the meat up and put it in the fridge, walking to the back door and letting Buddy out. He stepped onto the porch with the dog, noticing that clouds had moved in rapidly, as they were prone to do in the mountains. Tyler raised his head as he caught the scent of the coming rain, the smell so much stronger and more potent than he ever remembered it being. He could almost feel the storm riding in on the wind that had begun to blow and raised his head against the wind, feeling it blow through his short hair and his slowly growing beard. Looking over, he saw Buddy acting in a similar manner, his tail slightly wagging as Tyler felt the pure energy of the storm flowing through his body.

The smell of cooking meat suddenly overpowered the rain and Tyler returned to the kitchen to flip his burgers, finding himself literally drooling at the sight of the meat cooking, blood running out into the pan as the outside seared to a gray-brown color. He turned to the table and dove back into the bag of chips, shoving an entire handful into his mouth as he felt the hunger in his stomach demand food. He ate three more large handfuls before he had to force himself to go outside to distract himself from the smell of the meat. As he crossed the threshold of the door he was instantly met with another scent, not as strong as the rain, but lying just beneath it. Buddy had evidently caught the scent as well and he turned to the edge the forest, wagging his tail. Tyler was overtaken with the small hint of smell, knowing somehow that he recognized it. He couldn't figure out how, but he knew he'd smelled it before. He caught the sound of rustling in the woods once the wind had died down and instantly turned his eyes to the area the sound had come from. Buddy did the same, trotting down the stairs and standing at the edge of the yard as he looked for the source. Tyler caught the figure first.

"Hey," he shouted as he noticed the shadow of someone standing just inside the tree line. "What are you doing out there," he shouted, going to the bottom of the stairs.

The shadow moved as he approached, quickly ducking and retreating. Anger filled him as he thought of someone standing in the forest spying on him. He darted forward, rushing past the dog as he caught sight of the shadow quickly darting between trees deeper in the woods. He burst into the foliage, the scent much stronger here and walked slowly, expecting an attack from whoever was stalking him. His eyes adjusted to the darkness quickly, allowing him to see the trampled grass from where the person had stood there watching him. He stood cautiously, listening intently, seeing and hearing nothing. Whoever had been here was either very far away, or had stopped moving to watch him again. He backed slowly out of the woods and into his yard, his hunger screaming at him to eat. Turning, he trotted by the dog who now looked forlorn and confused, and went inside to eat his dinner.

He grabbed a plate and started to put hamburger buns in it, but once he caught sight of the food he found this to be ridiculous. He paused long enough to throw some cheese on the hot burgers before scooping them into the plate and killing the heat. He went to his table, the kitchen door still open to let in the fresh air, and sat down to enjoy his meal as he looked out at the coming storm. He grabbed his fork as he heard the first of the rain drops begin slapping the dead leaves, a cacophony of sound rising from the bottom of the mountain as the storm made its way up to his yard. He dug the fork into the meat and pulled a chunk free, almost moaning as he saw the red interior of the burger, blood dripping from his fork. He shoved the hot food into his mouth, shivering when he felt and tasted the bloody, rare meat cover his tongue. He quickly put another forkful of the delicious meat into his body.

Tyler lost himself in his meal. He felt the storm racing up the mountain, the wind rushing into his house, upsetting papers and curtains and anything it could get hold of while he ate. His eyes, when they weren't closed from sheer ecstasy, darted between his blood-filled plate and the darkening world outside his open door. It was the first rumble of thunder that made him aware of his surroundings again. He blinked as his eyes adjusted to the dark room after the lightning faded. He looked down at his plate and saw chunks of meat swimming in a pool of blood. He felt the hot, sticky blood running down his chin, all the way down his neck, soaking the neckband of his shirt. He had dropped his fork at some point, electing to eat the meat with his hands, ripping it apart and shoving hunks of it into his mouth like an animal. He looked at his blood covered hands in the menacing darkness, jumping up from the table as, for an instant, they appeared to be little more than blood covered claws. He took the plate and sat it on the porch, Buddy coming over to eat the minimal scraps that were left before lapping up the remainder of the grease and blood. Tyler ran to the sink and washed his hands and face, unable to get the water hot enough to clean himself to his own satisfaction.

What was happening to him? Had he really just done that? He shivered in the warm house as the wind blew the cold mist of the storm into the kitchen, a moderate patch of water drops already on the floor just inside the door. He stepped outside to watch the storm again, hoping the fresh air would bring some clarity to his throbbing head. He breathed deeply, at first smelling nothing but blood and grease, realizing it had somehow gotten onto his nose -

perhaps even in his nostrils. He hoped beyond hope that he hadn't plunged his face into the plate as Buddy had done. Lightning lit up the evening sky, thunder cracking so loud he seemed to feel it rumble in his very bones. The wind carried the scent of ozone and rain to his nostrils, accompanied once more by the other, familiar scent. He stared out into the darkness, trying to see where the man was this time as his eyes adjusted in the lightning's aftermath. After looking for a moment he pinpointed the hunched shadow again, the anger rising once more in his body as he took a breath to demand the man show himself. As he was about to speak lightning flashed once more, illuminating the world as bright as the noonday sun, giving Tyler a clear view of the man in the woods before the figure had a chance to retreat. He backed up slowly, stepping inside and slamming the door on the image that he knew couldn't exist. He couldn't rid himself of the sight that the lightning had given him however, and he soon ran upstairs to his bedroom and slammed his door in an attempt to get away from the sight of his father looking at him from the foliage.

***

Tyler took off the wet, bloody shirt and unbuttoned his pants, emptying his pockets in time to feel his phone vibrate. He cursed himself as he checked it, seeing five messages from Amy. They ranged in tune from moderately chipper to worried, the last one asking him if he needed her. He quickly texted her back, stating that the storm had caught him unawares and he had forgotten to check his phone. He wanted badly to tell her of his strange experience, knowing if there was one person in the world he could tell it would have to be her, but he couldn't bring himself to do it. He knew she was already worried enough about him without adding this to the list. Besides, she had elected to take care of Kayla rather than stay with him, so why should she care what was going on with him?

He caught himself as this thought filled his brain, unsure where it had come from. He had no idea what was going on with him and had to admit that he was more than a little scared. He stood from his bed, deciding that a nice hot shower would help straighten his head out. He stepped into the shower, the warm water soothing his skin as he'd hoped. He turned the water up slowly, waiting to reach the threshold just below scalding, which was how he loved to shower. He turned the water up a little at a time, seeing and feeling the steam, but still not feeling it was hot enough. He turned the knob until it wouldn't turn anymore, still unsatisfied with the temperature of the water. He chalked it up to the storm somehow interfering with his water until he looked at his skin and saw that every inch of his body was blood red and nearly smoking it was so hot. He stepped back, suddenly aware that the air in the bathroom had been replaced almost entirely with steam. He turned the water down a bit, hoping to cut through the steam, and grabbed the soap, knowing he needed to get the grease off of his face and neck. He washed himself quickly, rinsing his entire body with the scalding water before the first cramp hit.

He had just rinsed his hair when he felt his stomach clench a bit, instantly blaming the raw meat making its way through his system. He reached out to turn off the water and was forced to his knees by another clench of his stomach. It felt like his entire abdomen was twisting in on itself, trying to rip free of his body. Was this food poisoning? His body was wracked by another spasm of his insides, causing him to cry out. What the hell was going on? He reached up and pulled the curtain back, rolling out of the shower and onto his bath mat where he lay curled in a ball as the pain spread from his stomach to his chest, every organ, every muscle felt it was trying tear itself apart. Tears, white hot against his face, spilled from his eyes as he tried to crawl from the bathroom. His mind was so skewed by the pain he was barely able to form a coherent thought. He tried to make his way to the phone, sure if he could call Amy she could help.

At the thought of Amy he seemed to lose himself entirely, his mental image of the beautiful woman he was falling madly in love with being replaced by the image of the she-wolf in his dream emerging from the ruins of her body. This image made his heart skip a beat, his body becoming instantly aroused as he tried to understand what was happening. He realized two things at the same time as he entered the bedroom. First, he understood that the storm has stopped, and second he realized that he wasn't alone in the room.

***

Tyler heard the growling from the doorway, bringing him back to reality for a moment. He turned his head and looked Buddy in the eye, seeing the dog clearly despite the pitch black room. Buddy was hunched over in the doorway, his body rigid, every hair on his back standing at attention as he bared his teeth, a gesture Tyler couldn't imagine would be anything short of threatening. He tried to speak to the dog, his voice coming out as a cross between a moan and a growl. Buddy backed out into the hallway as Tyler crawled towards him, not even realizing he was going to do so. The closer he got to the dog, the louder the animal's growls became until his back paws met the edge of the stairs. Tucking his tail between his legs, the dog turned and ran down to the first floor, where he barked at Tyler from a distance.

Tyler's limbs seemed to have a mind of their own. He tried to draw in on himself as the pain spread throughout his entire body, but he kept crawling instead. He made it down three stairs before a terrible spasm shook his body, causing him to tumble headfirst down the rest. He landed at the bottom, a burning mess of pain. He looked at his arms and found himself growing even more confused. Thick brown hair had covered his forearms, making it look as though the bones themselves were changed. He turned himself back over, looking over his body and seeing the same thick hair covering his torso. As he watched he felt a particularly intense spasm of pain and saw his rib cage distend, the bones snapping and grinding against one another before fusing back together in a new shape, his skin splitting while blood ran down and matted the thick brown fur that emerged. He attempted to scream, emitting a thin, growling whine from a throat that seemed almost blocked, his vocal cords paralyzed. As his throat felt thicker his respirations doubled so could get enough oxygen. He felt the same grinding pain in his legs and forced his neck to twist around and watch as his tibia shattered and bent, reforming to resemble the leg of the dog that was now barking urgently from in front of him. He lurched forward, knowing he had to stop the dog's barking as he felt a surge of anger flood his brain.

The back door flew open when he got within reach of Buddy, a familiar voice ringing out in the dark house as he continued to writhe in pain and hatred.

"Jasper, out," the figure from the woods said firmly.

Tyler tried to reach out and grab the leg of the man who burst into his life after leaving it so long ago. His hand caught the edge of the man's pant leg and he grasped it tightly, feeling a sense of triumph as he drew himself closer to the intruder. Gently, but swiftly the man pulled his pants out of Tyler's grasp, causing him to roll over on his back and look up in agony. He caught a look that he would have sworn was a cross between sorrow and pity cross his father's face while he growled up at the man, doing his best to threaten the life of his elder.

"I'm sorry, Tyler," he said, before running out into the night, leaving the door open.

Tyler heard him calling out for Jasper, heard the two of them crashing off through the underbrush in the darkness. He felt more pain than he ever thought possible, now feeling as if his spine was being removed through his anus. As he tried to move, he felt an unfamiliar sensation on the back of his legs. It took him a few seconds to realize what he was feeling was the tail that had just emerged from the bottom of his spinal column. As he reached for something to help him make it to his feet, he saw the bones of his hands begin to shatter, extend and reform to make a paw identical to the ones the thing that attacked him had. He tried as hard as he could to wake up as he felt the pain move from his body to the center of his face, hoping beyond hope this was just another nightmare. Tyler screamed, roared in pain as his mandible snapped in two pieces and reformed, extending from his face to create an unmistakably canine snout. He felt his eyes and ears alter as well, his vision becoming even sharper as a million new smells attacked his snout at once. He pulled himself to his feet as the pain came to an end

Rage unlike anything he had ever felt filled his body. He looked around the house, feeling as if he was a witness to his actions rather than the one performing them. He tried to test this, attempting to make his arm move, with no luck. He felt the hatred running his body, filling his mind, and he felt more helpless than he ever had before. He caught the scent of the dog and the man drifting to him from miles away and his body launched out the door in pursuit of them. Tyler had no idea what was going on, but he said a prayer in his head as he felt his body, now running purely on anger and pain, dashing through the forest, growling deep in its throat as it did. He felt bits of his skin that clung to the fur drop from his body as thorns and weeds slapped and ripped at him as if angry at his presence.

Tyler was along for the ride as the wolf that took over his body raced through the dark woods, thoughts of murder and bloodshed filling its mind. The scent of the man and the dog faded as they went deeper into the woods, causing the thing to grow angrier. Tyler found himself loving it when the wolf stopped, stood and roared into the sky, feeling his own stresses slip away so much that he gave in and tried to howl to the moon with it, beyond shocked when his body obeyed his commands. He looked around with his eyes, dropping to all fours and feeling a hunger even greater than the one he had satisfied earlier before the wolf took over again, running forward as a new scent filled the night. They burst through the trees and practically tripped over the source of this new smell. The huge black bear stood on it hind legs and roared at him as it sensed the threat of the unfamiliar new creature that had just been plopped down in its presence.

The wolf stood on Tyler's hind legs, roaring back at the bear so fiercely that the animal, nearly as big as the wolf was itself, dropped back to all fours and began to waddle away. Tyler felt satisfaction at this, thinking the encounter was done, being awestruck as the wolf bounded after the bear and leapt onto its back, digging long claws into the bear's hide before rolling forward and pulling it down onto its side. Tyler felt true sorrow for the bear as it groaned out in anger and pain. He threw all of his effort into making the wolf back off and leave the old animal alone, telling his body to turn away and go back to his safe, familiar house. He had actually made his body turn and walk a few paces before he felt anger and hatred and hunger all race into his brain, taking over his body again and launching it at the bear. The fight was shorter than he feared, and caused more pain than he wanted. He felt the bear's teeth and claws pierce his sides and arms many times, as his own tore into the bear time and time again. Finally, once it had tired of the fight, the wolf stood on all fours and grabbed the bear by the snout, inserting its claw like fingers into the bear's mouth and grabbing the bottom of its jaw with the other hand. Tyler knew what it had planned and tried to stop it, but it was too late. The wolf ripped the bear's head in two, blood flying through the air, the bear's body let out an involuntary groan of pain and anguish as the dying brain utilized its last connection to the body before giving in altogether.

Tyler blacked out not long after this. He watched the death of the bear, feeling shock like nothing he had ever experienced accompanied by something that he would later only be able to liken to triumph and pride. He watched as the wolf bent his face down, seeing as his own jaws tore into the flesh of the bear, tasting the blood and meat that reminded him eerily of his dinner from earlier. The last thing Tyler saw that night was his own blood soaked, wolfish hands ripping into the body of his first victim.

***

He awoke the next morning, feeling the warmth of the sunlight on his skin before he quite registered its presence on his face. His entire body was in agony. Every nerve, every muscle, every bone all felt as though they'd been chewed up and spat out. He had no idea where he was, or why he felt so exposed. He reached up, somehow surprised he could move his own arms. He found a piece of cloth over his face as the wooden slats against his muscles told him that he was on the bench on his porch. He pulled the cloth off of his face, groaning when the sunlight hit his eyelids, sending twin needles of pain through his head. He opened his eyes slowly, looking around at his porch. How the hell did he end up out here? He looked down at his body and saw that it was covered in dirt and blood and bits of what looked like fur. He closed his eyes and tried to remember what happened. He could remember the storm racing up the mountain, his bloody hamburgers, his scalding shower. He remembered Buddy growling at him as he had stomach cramps. Could the fur be Buddy's? Did the dog attack him?

He stood slowly, looking around his porch for any sign of how he had gotten back. A large claw mark stood out on the post at the head of the porch stairs. Bloody footprints led to the bench and to the door, the boots that had made them sitting on the mat just outside. He thought he recognized them and knelt down, looking closer at them only to realize that he was right. The boots were his own. He stood up again, looking all around him yet again, trying to figure out what in the world was going on. His heart began to beat faster in his chest as he slowly opened the door, somehow feeling like an intruder in his own house. Silence filled the house as he crept inside, looking for any sign of anyone else.

The kitchen seemed to be straight, everything as he remembered leaving it the night before. As he got closer to the living room he saw something that stopped his heart. In the doorway between the living room and kitchen were a pair of clearly shredded pants lying in the floor right beside a large claw mark on the door frame. He crept closer to the doorway, suddenly maddeningly aware that he wasn't wearing a stitch of clothing. He heard a snort from the living room, followed by the sound of footprints trotting to the doorway. Unsure of what to expect, Tyler crouched, ready to either run or take action. Buddy came around the corner, tail rigid, looking warily at Tyler. He sniffed the air deeply before giving his tail a few quick wags and returning to the living room. Tyler walked to the doorway, peeking around to see Buddy laying in front of the couch, licking the hand of someone who was laying on his furniture.

"Come on in, Tyler," the man said, making Tyler jump.

"Dad? Is it really you?"

"In the flesh," the man said, sitting up. "What's left of it, anyway."

"What the hell is going on?"

"Nothing easy to explain, I'm afraid."

"Where have you been?"

"All over. But I always end up back here."

"Here? In the Smokies?"

"Yes."

"Why?"

"The same reason you did. That's where it feels at home."

"It?"

"The wolf, son. The wolf."

"Dad, I'm so confused."

"I know. One step at a time. First you need to text or call Amy."

"How do you know about Amy?"

"Well, for one I've watched you lately. And two, I've been keeping her sane as best I can."

"What do you mean?"

"You had about 20 messages from the girl when I made it back here last night. She was going to leave Kayla and come check on you. I told her your power had failed and your phone died."

"Thanks for that, I guess. Where's the phone?"

"Charging in the kitchen. If you want some privacy I can go outside."

"I'll just go upstairs. I need some clothes anyway."

"Alright," his father said, standing and stretching. Tyler was ashamed to see the saggy, dirty underwear his father was wearing, the man's own scrawny, gaunt body covered in a layer of dirt and blood comparable to his own.

"Help yourself to anything here, dad," he said as he grabbed his phone and walked up the stairs and into his bedroom. He climbed into the shower and washed the grime off of his body, hoping he would not find any open wounds that the dirt could have gotten into. He was unsurprised to find that this shower was similar to the one from the night before. He couldn't get the water hot enough to satisfy himself despite the excessive amount of steam and his own red skin. Once he'd cleaned himself, he ventured back into the bedroom and lay on his bed, relishing the fact that he could still smell a hint of Amy on the sheets. He pulled his phone over and brought her name up, looking at the messages his father had sent to calm her down.

He had told her about the power, apologized, told her he was fine and asked about Kayla. Not bad. He had even told her he loved her and he was looking forward to seeing her. Tyler would have to thank the man again, once he figured out what the hell was going on that is. He pushed the button to call her and prepared to discuss the night as best he could. She answered on the first ring, sounding both excited and nervous to hear from him.

"Tyler," she said almost breathlessly.

"Hey, beautiful," he said, feeling elated at hearing her voice after the hellish night.

"Are you OK?"

"Yeah, I'm good. A little tired, but not terrible. I miss you like crazy."

"I miss you, too."

"How did you ladies do last night?"

"Well…"

"What's wrong," he said, instantly nervous at the tone of her voice.

"Nothing right now…"

"OK?"

"Kayla had some sort of weird experience."

"What kind of experience?"

"She says she saw Doug."

"What?"

"I know. She says she saw him looking into her window, but it wasn't him."

"It was but it wasn't?"

"She wasn't making much sense."

"How is she now?"

"Nearly hysterical. This only happened at like 6."

"Tell me exactly what happened."

"She said she was looking out the window and she started to doze off. She opened her eyes and he was standing there looking in the window at her with tears in his eyes. She said she could barely recognized him. He was scarred up and his face was terribly thin. She said he looked like some kind of monster."

"Wow. That's rough."

"You're telling me. I need to ask something."

"Anything."

"I don't think she should be alone…"

"Of course. Babe, you stay as long as you need. She's your friend and she needs you."

"Thank you for being so sweet. I'm sorry all of this is happening."

"It's not your fault. Don't apologize. Just promise me something,"

"Anything,"

"Don't go anywhere without that gun in your hand."

"You've got it. Anything else?"

"Yeah. One more."

"OK?"

"Come back to me safe when this is all over?"

"You've got it, honey."

"I love you, Amy."

"I love you, too, Tyler. I'll talk to you soon, OK?"

"Look forward to it."

Tyler hung up the phone, feeling relieved that he didn't have to explain everything to Amy just yet, but still unable to shake the guilt of hiding something like this from her. She had her hands full with Kayla, though. There was no sense in making her worry about both of them. Besides, telling her he had turned into a wolf monster and his father had appeared like magic probably wouldn't make her want to stick around.

"It figures," he thought, feeling sorry for himself. "I finally get a good thing going and my life goes to crap."

He rolled to his feet, put on some clothes and walked down the stairs where his father was busy preparing breakfast in his skivvies.

"Dad?

"Yeah son?"

"I know there's some weird crap going on here, but would you like to shower, put on some clothes?"

"I would love that more than you realize. I just didn't bring any."

"Take whatever you want from the closet. I have some stuff that may fit you. Even though it doesn't seem to fit me right now," he said, tugging at the shirt that now seemed to hug his torso.

"That happens at first. The way I understand it can stay that way, if you embrace it."

"Embrace what?"

"It's a long story. I'll tell you what I know after I shower and we eat. OK?"

"Sure."

"How's Amy?"

"Worried. She wants to stay with Kayla. She said Kayla thought she saw our boss outside of her window."

"That's a bit creepy."

"More than creepy, actually. Doug died last week."

"Oh. That fella."

"Yeah. How did you know?"

"Like I said, I've been keeping an eye on you lately."

"You have?"

"Yes. I felt I had to."

"Why."

"Because you came here. Once I realized that I knew I had to try to keep you safe."

"Safe from what, Dad? What is going on down here?"

"Me. "

Tyler was stunned. What did the man mean? How and why would he have to be protected from his own father?

"What are you talking about?"

"It's a very long story, son. There is a lot your mother and I couldn't bring ourselves to tell you. I tried to keep this from you for your entire life."

"What? Keep what from me?"

"The wolf."

Tyler and his father looked at each other for a long time before either moved. The younger man felt his body going numb as the nightmares of the previous week played out before his eyes Flashes of memories from the night of his attack flashed through his mind, before finally settling on the wolf that had attacked him. In an instant every memory of last night flooded back to him as he felt the wolf tear through his flesh and fight for freedom. He dropped to his knees in the kitchen floor, feeling the pain all over again. He could feel the rage he had experienced at his father's presence. He felt his hands rip into the flesh of the bear he'd just murdered, tasted its stringy, tough flesh between his teeth. He felt chunks of meat and fur slide down his throat. Tyler's reverie was broken by the insane urge to vomit, as if that would purge his body of the things he had ingested against his will. He threw up in the trash can his father had just placed in front of him, appalled to find that there was indeed more than just his previous night's dinner in the can when he finished. He looked at the half-digested mess, unable to believe his eyes as he saw large hunks of thick, black fur floating in the mess. He heaved again, retching up more of the fur before his body relaxed again. He closed his eyes against the sight of his regurgitated meal and heaved once more, bringing nothing but pain this time.

Tears streamed down his face as he leaned back, wiping his face on the cold rag his father placed on his forehead. He heard his father walk slowly up the stairs, leaving him alone with his thoughts. He slowly let his mind drift back to what had happened last night. He felt his body tense as he remembered the sensation of something inside of him trying desperately to tear out. He clenched his fists as he remembered the claws sprouting from the ends of his slowly elongating fingers. He saw himself bounding through the darkened forest, his eyes and ears keener than ever before, able to see and sense the slightest movement from the forest around him. His body was covered in sweat by the time he was able to free himself of the memories of the night. He had no idea what could explain the terrible things in his mind. Could he really have been possessed by whatever this monster was?

"Tyler," his father said from the bottom of the stairs, bringing him out of the doze he hadn't even realized he'd slipped into.

"Yeah, Dad?"

"I'm more sorry than I can tell you. You have to know that."

"Sorry for what, Dad?"

"For all of this. It's my fault."

"How?"

"It's a curse."

"A what," Tyler said, feeling a hint of anger arise within him as the man who had been absent for most of his life used such a stupid excuse for his current pain.

"A curse. Passed through generations in a way that I don't even fully understand."

"Dad, I've heard a lot of stupid stuff in my life, but this takes the cake. You didn't want to be around, so you weren't. That's it. Don't try to cover your ass with something so senseless."

"Tyler, I'm being serious."

"Yeah? Well, go grab the Easter Bunny and tell your bull to him. I'm not listening."

"Son, please. Aren't you a little curious about what happened to you last night? What happened in the forest three days ago?"

"How do you know about that," he said, sitting bolt upright, a sudden spur of hatred flooding his brain before being replaced with confusion and fear.

"I was there, son. I'm sorry to admit it, but I was."

"Where? How? Why didn't you help me for God's sake?"

"I tried. Just like I'm sure you tried to avoid killing last night. But once the wolf is fully in control it's nearly impossible to break free."

"What are you saying?"

"It was me, Tyler. I was the wolf. It was all me."

Tyler felt his stomach clench again, his body suddenly wracked with more dry heaves as he processed the information his father had just given him. Suddenly he felt connections sliding into place. His father had been the wolf, had tried to kill him, and had somehow changed back after being stabbed and carried him back to his car, undressed him and left him there for Amy to find. He ran his hands through his hair as he thought of this, realizing that his father must have been the one who had brought his boots to the back door, actually he hadn't just brought them. He'd worn them. He turned his head back to the shredded clothes by the doorway to the kitchen, finally recognizing them as being his own from that night.

"You were the wolf?"

"Unfortunately, I was. I'm so sorry, Tyler. I can't tell you how much it hurts me to admit this to you. We thought you were safe from it if I wasn't around, but it led you here anyway."

"Slow down. What are you talking about? I deserve an explanation here, Dad. You're absent for most of my life and now suddenly you come back into the picture, let yourself into my house twice, break into my dreams, and now you tell me you are some kind of wolf monster that attacked me and ruined my life?"

"Son, I'm- hold on, what? What do you mean broke into your dreams?"

"I've been dreaming about you and some big wolf monster for days. Before I even actually saw it."

"Please tell me about these dreams."

Tyler paused a moment, debating on making the man leave, before deciding to just indulge him. He started the story with hearing his father's voice on the radio and ended with wrecking his car.

"So you dreamed of me turning into a wolf before ever actually seeing the wolf?"

"Yes."

"And Kayla thinks that Doug killed her dog?"

"Yes. But that's just trauma. She's torn up about his death. She only thinks that because the cops lost his body."

"They what? The body is gone?"

"Yeah. They said they put it in the drawer and didn't check it for a few days and when they tried to do the autopsy it was gone."

"Oh God. How did he die?"

"He swerved off a mountain road and was ejected from the car."

"Oh God. Are you sure he wasn't attacked by anything?"

"All the cops told us is that he ran off the ridge, was thrown out and crushed and that some animal had found him before they did."

"Tyler this is much more dangerous than I'd thought."

"What is? You still haven't told me a damn thing," he said, slamming his fist into the floor hard enough to shake the glasses in the kitchen cabinet, causing the dog to draw his lips back and growl deeply.

"Jasper, sit," his father said before turning to Tyler again. "I know I haven't. I really don't know where to begin. It's so overwhelming. But you have to know all I can tell you before nightfall."

"Yes. I do. But, the dog is yours?"

"Jasper? Yeah. He came to you about a week ago, right?"

"Jasper? We've been calling him Buddy. Yeah. He showed up the night I had the second dream."

"That's what I thought."

"How is all of this possible, Dad? How did I dream about you, hear your voice on the radio, and how is all of this real?"

"The only explanation I have for the first two is that we are connected, of course. It is a blood curse. I had a bit of a similar experience from my father before it happened, but nothing like what you've had."

"Before what happened?"

"Before he bit me. Before he passed the curse down to me. I need to start from the beginning. As much of it as I know at least."

"Please do. Because I don't know how much more of this I can wrap my head around without an explanation."

"Very well. Here is what I know. Our family comes from a long line of people who called themselves Sin Eaters. They believed that they could literally take on the sins of others by eating from a full plate of food that was placed on a dead or dying person's chest and prayed over. I don't know exactly when or why it started, but this was who they were, who they lived to be. They kept their faces covered in public when performing this service so no one would know exactly who they were, allowing them to live normally. It was tradition for the son to take on the sins of his father as the man died, thus taking on the role of sin eater for the community they lived in. One young man in our family history didn't want to do that.

The family had moved to the Smokies in the early 1900's to be farmers, occasionally finding work with the local loggers to make extra money while they hid their calling from their neighbors. Well, as the elder man grew sick he called upon his son to take the mantle up and serve the people as he had. The boy refused. He severed all ties with his family and left, travelling down the river and settling down and building his own farm. The father fought his illness for over a year before succumbing to it. His death rocked the son, but not as much as what came after it. The man, it would seem, didn't stay dead."

"How is that possible?"

"Well, a lot of cultures have legends about someone who dies with a great burden, or with unfinished business being unable to rest. One of the legends I've been able to find in our family's history warns that one who dies with sins on his soul, without the ritual being performed correctly, will be unable to rest and will walk for eternity, tormenting those he loved in life."

"What ritual? And what happened?"

"I don't know many details of the ritual, other than the basic knowledge of sin eaters did. I know the father who did not get the benefit of the ritual came back with the wolf. His body was possessed by a restless spirit that targeted the one who was supposed to free him of his burden. It tracked the boy to his new farm on the side of a mountain, his closest neighbors miles away, and attacked him one night when the moon was at its peak, when the wolf is strongest.

"The attack allowed the spirit of the wolf to pass from father to son, freeing the old man's body and taking over the young farmer. The burden of sin in spiritual form resided within his body for three days, tormenting him and slowly preparing his body for the change. He ate ravenously, he became stronger, angrier. To make a long story short, he attacked many people until he turned. Then he went on a rampage.

"What kind of rampage?"

"The wolf took over fully. Once his body experienced the change, it happened nightly, usually riding the cycle of the moon, but he could even change when the moon was covered. The bite always spread the spirit, making more people feel the effect of his unwillingness to take his position, but never leaving them as enslaved as he was.

"The wolf tore at him for nearly two decades before tiring of him. When his body was nearly broken from the experience, he found his eldest son and passed it on to him. This continued for generations. The eldest son typically only got the bite on a blood moon when the wolf was ready to move on. With the family legends long since lost, no one really knew how to stop it. Five times in the last 100 years the curse has been passed down through our family. My father's father was the first to go back and try to uncover the truth. He found out enough that he was able to warn his eldest son. My father sat me down when I was a teenager and explained things to me. I thought him a fool at first. He had me tie him up in the hopes that it would show me what he meant.

"Nothing happened. I think the wolf knew what he was trying. My father wanted me to end it. I tied him up the two nights leading up to a blood moon and sat up with him, thinking he was going crazy. He begged me to tie him up on the third night. He said he could feel it inside of him, growing restless and angry. He told me he wanted to end the curse once and for all. He believed if I killed him on the night of the blood moon while the wolf had taken over it would not only stop the curse and save me, but he believed it would release everyone who had ever gotten the bite.

"I refused, like I said. I was out with your mother when I first heard the howl. I made up a story about being sick and took her home, kissing her for what I thought might be the last time. I pulled the gun I'd gotten for my birthday out of the trunk and drove home through the outskirts of the city where we lived. I don't know what I expected, but I know it wasn't what happened. The wolf jumped onto my car and ripped through the roof. I had a ragtop muscle car, of course. It was the 80's after all. It grabbed me by the head and pulled me out of the car as we went skidding off the road. I felt our bodies get thrown through the air as the car crashed into a tree. My back hit the same tree, our bodies bouncing away as I felt my spine snap.

I tried to crawl away when we landed, but I couldn't move my legs. I watched as the wolf slowly healed in the red moonlight. I will never forget the sound of its crushed rib cage re-inflating and rebuilding itself as I watched, mist rising from its skin like a cold stream when the sun hits it. I was frozen to the spot, partially due to my literal paralysis and partly to fear. It crawled over to me on legs that were still bent at awkward angles, so eager for the hunt that it couldn't wait. I tried to scream as its mouth closed over my throat, but I couldn't. I began choking on my own blood as its fangs tore into my esophagus. When I finally remembered that I had the pistol I put it up to the thing's head and fired. I felt its brains and bits of its skull splatter on my face as I struggled to breathe.

I turned my head as the world went black to see the face of my father, smiling in peace before I passed out. I thought I was dead. When I woke up, the first thing I saw was sunlight. It had been late when I dropped your mother off and I knew it hadn't been more than a few hours since I'd been attacked. I planned on laying there until the police came to arrest me as I laid beside my dead father, the murder weapon still in my hand. I turned over onto my side before I realized that I had no pain. My neck felt fine, I could move my legs and my back had stopped throbbing. I stood quickly, terrified that I had been slipped some sort of drug and had a hallucination that had literally left me to kill my own father. It only took one glance down at my blood soaked shirt, the claw marks in the chest and on my jeans to make me sure it wasn't false."

"What did you do," Tyler whispered slowly.

"The only thing I thought of. I grabbed the biggest branches I could find, apologized to my father, and covered his body with them. I ran to my car, feeling more blessed than you can imagine that it would start and drove away. I drove the car into the worst part of the city and waited for someone to come along and strip it before reporting it stolen. I caught Hell from my mother for skipping school after your mother called to ask if I was still feeling poorly. But I made it work. I felt the change as my father had said I would. I began to crave meat. I ate four steaks in one sitting the night after the attack. My mother chalked it up to grief over my father, who had turned up missing. On the third night I left the house and went to where my father's body was. No one had found him yet and I could smell the decomposition before I even reached the right road. The wolf tore my body apart that first night, much like it did yours. It's always that way the first couple of times. Unable to stop myself, I watched as the wolf approached the one thing that was familiar to it on that road. I watched as it gorged itself on the remains of my father."

Silence filled the room as Tyler processed this information. Could this be real? He had just been told that he was the victim of an at least century old curse and that his father had literally eaten his grandfather. He closed his eyes as another wave of nausea hit. What was he supposed to do with this information?

"What comes next here?"

"What do you mean?"

"I mean, what do I do? If this is real and I've got some kind of wolf monster living inside of me, what am I supposed to do?"

"Live."

"How can I live like this?"

"It isn't easy, but it can happen. The wolf comes three to five nights a month, unless you call on it more often. Typically it doesn't affect your everyday life once you get used to the changes."

"What other changes are there?"

"Anger is the largest one. The wolf is fierce. It doesn't take anything to make you go completely over the edge."

"I already know about that."

"What do you mean?"

"I exploded on a guy yesterday before...whatever happened."

"Tell me everything."

Tyler explained the situation at the grocery store, making sure to give explicit details of the way the man had slammed into him with the buggy. He told his father that he knew he had to have burned his arm severely, describing the way he felt there must have been blisters on his skin that burst when he moved. He finished the story by telling of his lack of injury when he went to his car and Jasper's unpleasant reaction to sniffing the arm in question.

"You didn't actually see any blisters right after touching the metal, though?"

"Well no, I was too busy throwing a shopping cart and its user across the store."

"It could be that you didn't get as hurt as you thought, or..."

"Or what?"

"Or the wolf has taken hold in you much faster than in most cases."

"What do you mean?"

"Well, the injury accompanied by the transfer always heals almost as soon as the wolf settles into the body. The moonlight sees to that. But healing that quickly doesn't typically happen right away in my experience. For me it took months before I could even see a scrape heal faster than a few hours, much less a severe burn in a matter of minutes."

"What does that mean for me?"

"I have no idea, actually. I want you to tell me the rest of the night. Tell me everything you remember from the time Jasper sniffed your arm until you woke up this morning and found me here."

Tyler went through the whole thing, telling his father
everything that he remembered about the night from his
craving for bloody meat to waking up on the bench until he
remembered it all. He watched the man's reaction, seeing
his eyes widen at some points, while he frowned and
rubbed his chin at others. Could he be telling a story that
was unbelievable? After everything his father had told him,
could the man really be doubting his own account of the
night? Once he was finished he sat back and looked at his
father, still almost unable to believe that he was actually
there in the same room with the man he barely knew.

"This is all very unexpected," his father said after
sitting in silence for what felt like an hour.

"What do you mean?"

"Some of the things you've told me… you healed
unusually quickly, you had a craving that strong for meat,
and in the woods…"

"Well I've been craving meat on a certain level
since the attack, but it got worse every day until I felt
myself lose control yesterday. And what about the woods?"

"It has? The cravings, tell me about them."

"I've just wanted meat. I ate almost a pound of
bacon by myself the morning after the attack when I woke
up at Kayla's. Ever since then I've wanted nothing but
meat. What about the woods?"

"That's not exactly common. I didn't start craving
meat until after my first turn. I don't know what to make of
this."

"Dad," he said loudly, as the man sank into the
couch cushions, deep in thought, "what about the woods?"

"What? Right. You said that you were able to make
yourself, or the wolf, pause and stop what it was doing a
couple of times. You basically took control away from it.
Right?"

"Yeah, I guess. I was able to make it stop once
before it killed the bear. I made it start to walk away."

"That's amazing."

"Why? You said you could learn to live with the
wolf, or something, right?"

"Yes. After much time most people can learn to live with the wolf, can even figure out how to coax and guide it to do or not do certain things, but I've never seen a tale of someone actually stopping it altogether, even for a second. Especially not on the first turn. I've lived with it for over 30 years and I've never figured out how to do that."

Tyler laid down on the couch, his hands over his face, trying to make sense of everything. He didn't know if he should be more troubled about the situation or the man he had to rely on to help him face whatever was happening here. His father spoke more while he lay in silence, explaining that Buddy/Jasper had actually been his dog all along and that he had come to Tyler after feeling the unrest in the wolf and was vaguely familiar with him after keeping an eye on him. He listened as his father explained that the next two nights would be the hardest and that, after the wolf ripped him apart for these nights it would be truly one with his body and would be able to just transform from him, as he'd seen it do in his dreams.

"But how did I have those dreams," he asked, suddenly aware that he hadn't heard any explanation for that.

"I honestly don't know about that. I've never heard of anything like it. You saw me in clear detail, and you saw the wolf fully?"

"Yeah. Everything is just how I saw it. The way you have changed, the wolf, even the way it moves. I even saw claw marks around the cabin after having that dream."

"I was there," his father said, matter-of-factly. "That was the night I caught your scent as well as your boss, Doug's. I think I was actually following him the night he wrecked. I know that I was there afterward. I remember finding his body."

"And then what?"

"I'm not certain. The wolf can keep you from seeing things sometimes. Or maybe it's your own brain being unwilling to witness the Hell in front of your eyes. One way or the other, there are things that you can't remember at times."

"The police said that he had been partially eaten."

"You told me," his father said, catching a hint of his urgency.

"Does the bite affect someone who is dead?"

"No. But if they get it before they're dead... I've never heard of it, but I imagine it may be able to take hold."

"Doug disappeared within three days of being brought in."

"I remember."

"If someone else had the wolf, how could you still turn me? And how were you not turned last night?"

"Like I said, the bite can be spread. Others will get a weaker version of the spirit, and, of course, the more people who have it, the weaker it will be. There are tales in other countries of people who have it and learn to live with it for decades. It's the bite from father to son that passes the curse on, literally. It takes it from the original host and frees them, condemning the bitten. But anyone bitten on another night will get the curse as well, it just won't free the biter. These others burn themselves out quickly, the wolf uses their bodies during the full moon only, until their bodies or minds break from the pressure. That's where common werewolf stories come from. "

"What happens if you die after being bitten?"

"I don't know. Until today I would have thought you'd stay dead, but after hearing about Doug...I just don't know."

"Dad, do you think he could have been turned?"

"It's possible. If he was still alive when I, when the wolf, found him."

"What would he do?"

"The wolf always goes after those the human host loved. Typically this means family, which is why I stayed so far away from you as often as I could. It leeches on a person's humanity. That gives it insight into who that person loves, what they do, who they were. It also sometimes give the wolf strange characteristics. It can inspire some weird behavior. To avoid it all I left, you, your mother, Illinois. All of it. I still found myself in another state some mornings and had to find my way back."

"Doug doesn't have any family that we know of."

"No kids, ex-wife, parents, siblings?"

"Just a sick mother somewhere West of Tennessee."

"Significant other?"

"The closest he had to that was Kayla."

"And she says she saw him last night?"

"Yeah. And she is convinced he killed her dog the night you attacked me. That's actually why I was on the road that night. I was going to meet Amy there and help take care of Kayla."

"And Amy is still there now."

"Dad we have to go. We can't leave her there to be killed."

"I don't think she'll be killed. It's been three nights since he would have had his first change. I would say he's done turning. I've never known anyone to turn more than five nights in one month."

"You've also never known anyone to come back from the dead."

"That's also true."

"What if the wolf is the one in total control? What if dying caused the humanity to leave him, but the wolf survived? Maybe there is no Doug left. If there was, I'm sure he would have contacted one of us and tried to find out what happened."

"If the wolf is the one residing in his body then I have no idea what it would do. For that matter, I'm not even sure that puts it in the same category as everyone else afflicted with the curse."

"What do you mean?"

"I mean, if I had to guess, that this situation would make the wolf something new entirely. Humanity is usually what keeps the wolf moderately in check. If there is no more Doug in his body then he is all wolf. Worse, all wolf that can pose as a human. I have no idea what change that would allow in its behavior."

"We have to go to her," Tyler said, jumping to his feet.

"Hold on, son, you can't just go running over there right now."

"Why? I love Amy, Dad. I can't just leave her there."

"That's exactly why you can't go. You love her. If you know that, so does the wolf. If you go over there, you'll only ruin her life, maybe even take it from her. The sun is going to be setting soon and the moon will rise soon after."

"What do I do, then?"

"You just have to tell her to be ready for anything."

"They have guns."

"That won't do them any good."

"Why? What if they blow its brains out?"

"It won't work. It may slow the wolf down, but it won't kill it. Kayla may be able to take it out, but I don't know how strong her feelings for Doug were, or for that matter, how strong his were for her."

"Why does that matter?"

"Only a loved one can free you from the curse once you're under it."

"Seriously? Fairy tale crap?"

"Every myth has a basis in reality. It's the only way I can describe it."

"Describe what?"

"The only account I've ever seen of someone not cursed killing someone who is."

***

While waiting for his father to tell the tale, Tyler texted Amy and asked her to stay inside and have her things ready to go in case they needed to move. She questioned his request as he knew she would, but she told him she would do as he asked. Tyler's heart raced as Jack finally reached into a bag he hadn't noticed before, producing a journal he said had been passed down through their family.

"A journal," Jack said, "that gives an account of the sin eater's son who refused his father's ritual."

The journal, written by a man named Ben Randolph, gave a detailed account of the days leading up to his bite, as well as those leading to his transformation. Vague entries started when he began feeling separation from his family and their ideas, increasing when he left his father's home and went to a different part of the county to build his own. Within a year entries became more frequent as he wrote down the details of his father's illness, and the patriarch's insistence that his own sins should be consumed before it was too late. Ben wrote that he felt conflict he couldn't explain.

He had been raised understanding his father's beliefs and those of his extended family. The idea that sins must be consumed if a soul were to ever be able to enter Heaven is one that was pounded into his brain from the time he was old enough to understand it. But it was not a compulsion he shared. He felt there must be more to the story of this 'responsibility' than his father was willing to share. Maybe even more than he was aware of. The early entries in his journal went into detail about the way his ideas conflicted with those of his family.

"But the part that concerns us is a specific series of entries. Ben lived with the wolf for what appears to be a couple decades. He occasionally wrote of his belief about the creature living inside him, but his speculation eventually led him down a dark path. He embraced the wolf. He used its strength to build a life for himself and his growing family. But it wore him down fast. As his body started to wear down, the wolf turned on him. Ben was hit hard by the turn leading up to his own blood moon. He attacked surrounding farms for days as the wolf raged. The wolf even managed to fund its way to Ben's mother. It took her life in cold blood. His neighbors, all of whom depended on their farms for their livelihood, decided to find the beast that was behind the attacks."

Tyler flipped through the fragile pages his father pointed out to him, reading the first hand ravings of his ancestor that nearly sounded mad. He described a beast almost identical to the one Tyler himself had fought. A beast that, if all of this was true, was lurking inside the man sitting in his living room right now.

Randolph had been in town when he overheard his neighbors talking about the attacks on their farm. He was going to ignore the conversation and slip back into the shadow of the general store when he heard his name. They had heard his mother was dead and they were under the impression he'd gone to bury her. They figured the Randolph farm was the only one that hadn't been attacked yet and, rather than assume the worst about him, they assumed his house was next.

"That pretty wife of his will be there with the boy," Josiah Ramey said. "If she's there alone when it comes and nobody is there to help, there's no tellin' what ruin that man'll come home to. Just had his Ma die, he don't need to find his woman ripped to bits too."

It was decided. The men, a small hunting party, would depart from Ramey's place and make the short hike through the woods to Ben's farm that night - the night of the blood moon.

Ben had panicked, leaving his would-be purchases behind and rushing home to prepare. He knew the change that had taken place the previous few nights, and he could feel the same unrest again. He had stopped writing as the sun was sinking on the horizon, describing the rage and hunger flooding his body, leaving an apology to his wife and telling her he had to get away before it was too late.

Randolph's next entry had described a bloodbath. The wolf had broken loose when Tyler was just ten miles upriver and had rushed back to his home, meeting the hunting party in the woods. He described broken images of murder and mayhem in the forest, the wolf tearing men to shreds before the remaining few hunters had broken into the open field and fled for his house. The wolf followed.

Tyler's ancestor had written about seeing the men shooting at him as if it was a dream, feeling the bullets hit him as he attacked them. He described the feeling he had as the wolf ripped into the flesh of his friends and neighbors, the bloodlust that filled his very soul. But it was the image of his wife that alarmed his most. Karen had met the men in front of their home and refused to give them refuge. She met them with gun in hand and, when they were attacking the wolf, attacked them in turn.

His body was ravaged by bullets and buckshot, knife wounds and fists, eventually making him lose consciousness. As he lay on the ground on the edge of darkness, he saw a sight that chilled Tyler to the bone. Ben Randolph watched as his wife turned into a wolf.

As her body was being ripped apart by the beast within, his own body was returning to its human form. His eyes were going in and out of focus as the wolf that had been his wife stood tall and howled into the rainy night. Neither of them had noticed their son slipping outside. The twelve-year-old was unsure of what he had seen, but was certain his father lay wounded in front of a monster holding shreds of his mother's clothes. He didn't hesitate to grab the gun now lying on the ground and bring it up to the beast's face. Ben felt the rage inside the wolf battling with the love inside his wife's mind as they both fought for control. As the beast screamed at the youngest Randolph, the boy pushed the shotgun into its mouth and pulled the trigger. The entry had ended with three sentences.

She's dead. Karen is dead. I wish I had died, too.

***

"So, because the boy loved his mother, he was able to kill the wolf," Tyler asked slowly.

"That's the only thing I can assume."

"Did he even know she was the beast? Did Ben ever tell him?"

"The journal doesn't say," Jack told his son, taking back the old book. "I've looked for other accounts, even tried to see if young Sam had similar journal, but I've come up empty. For whatever reason the love the boy shared with his mother was enough to free her, and it has happened that way more times throughout the world."

"And that's the only way to kill one? A loved one freeing you?"

"Not necessarily."

"How else? Fire, guns, drowning?"

"Another wolf," his father said, slowly.

"How," Tyler said breathlessly, feeling his heart begin to accelerate as the sun sank toward the horizon. He could feel the anxious tension rising in his body, hunger mixed with hatred and anger churning in his stomach.

"Just attacking. Beheading is usually the easiest, but I imagine any sort of attempt should work. The wolves are like spirits, so it makes sense that they would cancel each other out. Plus the one who has inherited the stronger wolf should definitely come out on top. And if he doesn't, then the curse would end for the family, I should think."

"So what should I do?"

"What do you mean?"

"I inherited the stronger spirit, right? So what should I do to end it?"

"Nothing. Tyler, you don't begin to know how to handle yourself with the wolf inside of you, much less when it is in control. If this other wolf is in control of Doug without any of his human-self left, it would tear you apart, and if it didn't you'd tear Amy apart. It can't work."

"I controlled it last night."

"For a few seconds, Tyler. But it went right back and did what it wanted anyway, probably more violently than it would have otherwise. Besides, if there's nothing of Doug left to try and contain his wolf who knows how strong it is. It could rip the wolf in you to shreds without blinking for all we know. The wolf you have may be the purer spirit, but one without a human side could be a whole new problem that we can't begin to solve in one night."

"But it would give Amy time. It would give them a chance. I can't let her die for no reason. You have to see that."

"I understand son, I do."

"No you don't," Tyler said, leaping to his feet as the anger took over. "You left me alone, didn't tell me anything about this. You left me with a mother who cared more about her wine than her own son."

"Tyler, your mother loves you more than anything. So do I. She…"

"She what? What excuse do you have now," Tyler said, finding his eyes focusing on the small features of his father's face as the light faded from the room quickly.

"She loves you more than you'll ever know. She just had no idea how to raise you the way she had to. She knew about my condition and we tried to make sure we didn't have a child until I found a cure. But it didn't work."

Tyler felt his body hunch slightly as his muscles tightened. He knew the moon would be rising soon and he would become more angry and more dangerous. He took a deep breath and forced himself to calm down, unclenching his fists to see 8 small crescents of fresh blood on his palms. He watched as the wounds behind the droplets healed and wiped his palms on his pants, sitting on the edge of the couch as he forced the anger into the pit of his stomach, where it churned and roiled, making him almost nauseated with its urgency.

"Dad, I have to do something. One way or the other I'm going to turn tonight and if I can't get out of here I'll rip my house to shreds. It isn't much, but I do like the place. I would like to be able to try to stop Doug, if he is there."

"You don't even know if he is. Kayla is suffering right now, and she's been drunk both times she thought she needed to blame her problems on a dead man. This could just as easily be PTSD or something similar, Tyler."

"I can't take that risk. I love Amy and I'd die to protect her. I've never felt that way about someone and I can't let it go just because she might not be in danger. What if he is there and he rips her in half, or worse, bites her and spreads this to her, too."

"What if you do, Tyler?"

"You can make sure that doesn't happen."

"Son, I can't change. I'm done. It's done with me."

"No, but you can kill me if you have to. Or you can explain things to her and she can do it."

"What if she thinks I'm crazy and calls the cops? Or worse, what if she can't bring herself to do it?"

"Then I'll have to hope that I can stop the wolf enough to push it away myself."

"Tyler, please. Haven't enough people died because of this?"

"Yes. And I refuse to let Amy be one of them. I'm doing this, Jack. With or without you."

"Fine," he said, feeling almost proud to see a bit of his own stubborn attitude in his son as he stood and called for Jasper. "We'll drive over to Kayla's and try to explain this before it happens. You need to drive. I haven't in quite some time."

They piled into Tyler's car and raced down the road toward Kayla's home, the sun's last rays kissing the clouds before disappearing behind the mountains and leaving the sky in a growing state of darkness. They passed the spot where Tyler had wrecked his car as the first sign of the moon peered over the horizon. Tyler felt the wolf inside of him, writhing in hatred and struggling to break free. He held it back fiercely, gritting his teeth against the pain that wracked his body. His father looked over and saw the struggle that was going on in his son's body, instantly feeling fear flood his own. Tyler caught scent of the fear emanating from his father's every pore as he crested the hill and passed the place where his own fate had been written. He felt his limbs tense as his bones began to shatter and reshape themselves, his torso extending until it touched the steering wheel. He pressed the brake firmly and stopped the car, rolling out of the driver's side and into the road.

His father leaped out of the car and ran around to try and help him. The older man watched in horror as his son's limbs were broken and reconfigured, thick brown hair sprouting over every inch of his body. Tyler ripped at his skin and clothing, removing everything before it became too restrictive, allowing him to push himself away from his father and the car. He looked at the man in pain just before he felt his abdomen clench and his mandible snap, snarling one word that was barely intelligible in the midst of the wolf's growling with his vocal cords.

"Run."

Jack Randolph was frozen to the spot as he watched the transformation he'd only imagined playing out before his eyes. Hatred filled his son's eyes, flooding Jack's very mind as he realized the wolf still had some connection to his own body, and he fell to his knees in shock. The wolf stood, its face finishing the transformation as it ripped away the last of Tyler's skin and roared into the night. It turned on Jack, who was now crying silently by the still running car. It hunched over, raising one clawed hand over its head as if it meant to take off Jack's head. As Jack saw his life flash before his eyes he felt something rush past him, thinking for an instant that the strike had come without him even seeing it. Something dark and hairy slammed into the wolf's chest, knocking it back to the ground as Jasper rolled away, managing to dodge the teeth and claws that chased him. He stood between Jack and the wolf, barking viciously as the man leaped to his feet and dove into the driver's seat of the car, throwing it into gear and pressing the gas pedal, yelling for Jasper to run. The dog stood his ground as the wolf regained its footing and snarled in anger.

It ignored the car rolling away, looking after it once as Jack leaned out the window, calling for Jasper and turned to the dog, meaning to take its life before pursuing the old man. Tyler watched as his hands clenched into fists, the wolf rising to its full height again, while Jasper growled and crouched, waiting to pounce. He lurched forward, swinging his fist, the dog reacting quickly. Jasper jumped nearly straight up, dodging the wolf's blow and latching onto its throat, shaking his head viciously when he had dug his teeth in deeply.

Tyler felt the wolf's surprise mix with his own as the smaller canine began thrashing wildly, the skin ripping all around the wolf's throat. He found it harder and harder to breathe in the few seconds before the wolf grabbed Jasper around the ribs, one large paw centering at the sternum while the fingers almost met at the spine. It ripped Jasper away from its body, taking the majority of its throat with him and threw the dog like a ragdoll. The wolf's satisfaction filled Tyler's mind as they heard the thump and yelp of the dog hitting a tree in the darkness, followed by the sound of it sliding into the underbrush and lying still. The wolf struggled for breath for a moment as it pushed itself into the open and threw its head back, allowing the moonlight to fall on its wounds. Tyler felt the warmth of the light fall on his skin like that of the sun, his flesh knitting itself back together as the moonlight somehow allowed the wolf to heal.

He took a deep breath and faced the road ahead. He knew his father had gone ahead to warn Kayla and Amy of the danger that was coming their way. As this thought crossed his mind his body filled with anger again and he knew that the wolf had realized the same thing.

***

Amy and Kayla were sitting on the couch watching a horror movie, with only a lamp providing illumination for the large house. Why Kayla had insisted on a horror movie, Amy was unsure, but she didn't want to argue with her friend, knowing the woman had suffered more in the last week than anyone she'd ever known. The fact that she had been in ever increasing states of inebriation since dawn didn't make the idea of arguing about her choice in movies very appealing either. They were about halfway through the seventh or eighth sequel of a movie about a masked man slicing and dicing dumb college kids when someone began pounding on the door.

The women jumped and screamed, both instantly feeling foolish as they realized that masked murderers don't knock- and if one would happen to have such manners, they had certainly just sealed their doom and let him know they were in the house. Amy stood, against Kayla's pleas, reminding her that Tyler was still on his own and that the knocker could very well be him. She walked to the door, suddenly more nervous than she could understand and looked through the peephole. She watched as a fidgety, gaunt man looked around, wringing his hands as if terrified of something. He was about to knock again when she opened the door a crack and asked if she could help him.

"Amy," he said in a strained, raspy voice that she didn't recognize. "Or are you Kayla?"

"Who are you," she responded, unsure how the man would know both of their names.

"My name is Jack Randolph. I'm Tyler's father."

She stepped back in shock, opening the door more fully, turning the porch light on to get a better look at the small man making such a big claim.

"You're Tyler's father?"

"Yes. He sent me ahead to warn you. We all need to leave right now."

"What are you talking about?"

"Tyler is not himself right now. If you stay here, you will be in danger. Please believe what I am saying."

"How can I even believe that you are who you say you are? And even if you are his father, why would he send you ahead, and why should I trust you for a second?"

"The dreams were real, Amy. Tyler is not crazy and he is not wrong. The dreams were every bit as real as I am here. The wolf is not fake."

"How do you know about that," she said, suddenly angry that the man would throw Tyler's personal afflictions into the conversation as if that would change her mind.

"He told me. He told me everything, Amy. The wolf is real. It was me. I attacked him. I couldn't stop myself, but none of that matters now because the wolf is coming. It may already be here."

"What the hell are you talking about," Kayla said, stepping out of the living room and looking hard at the little man on her porch. "You attacked Tyler? If you're his dad why did you attack him? And what is the wolf? There aren't any wolves in the mountains."

"I don't have time to explain. Please. We are all in danger," he said as Kayla stepped forward and leaned out of the door, peering out into the darkness.

"I don't know if he's lyin' or not sweetie, but that's your man's car out there," she said as she looked around the strangely nervous man on her porch.

Amy peered around him and saw that she was right. The car was still running and the door was standing open, as if the man wanted to leave in a hurry.

"Yes, he sent me ahead like I said. He came here to warn you-" he started as a snarling growl came from the darkness, the thrashing of some large animal following it. "It's too late. Get back inside," he said, rushing forward and slamming the door behind him.

"Nobody invited you in, old man," Kayla said, as she grabbed the door frame in an attempt to regain her footing. "Now what the hell are you talking about?"

"Please get your guns. I'll tell you everything, but we need to be ready."

"How do you know we have guns?"

"Tyler told me. Please hurry," he said as the sound of growling approached the house. "We have to be able to defend ourselves."

"Against what?"

"Against Tyler. Now come on, please."

"Tyler? What about Tyler?"

"Amy there isn't time. The guns."

Kayla screamed as something slammed against the side of the house, growling at an all new level. Amy turned and ran, grabbing Kayla's shotgun from behind the couch, a box of shells in her hand. She tossed the shells to Jack and grabbed her purse, getting a box of bullets and her own .45 from inside.

"Tell me what's going on," she said, pocketing her bullets and pointing her gun at Jack while shouldering the shotgun.

"Amy, everything Tyler dreamed is real. The wolf is real. It is in him now, and he's out there, ready to come in here and rip us to pieces."

"How is it real?"

"If we make it through this he and I will tell you, but please, stop pointing that gun at me."

"Fine," she said, turning her gun on the door as Kayla backed slowly to the stairs and covered her ears, tears streaming down her face as she pleaded for safety. "Why would Tyler be trying to kill us?"

"Tyler isn't. It's the wolf. It comes after those its host loves most."

"And you think he's coming here?"

"I know he is. We were on the way here when he turned."

"Why?"

"We think Doug is a wolf, too."

Kayla heard this and stood up, her face hopeful. "Doug is alive?"

"No. If he has the wolf in him there is nothing left of Doug. I've never seen the curse go to someone who dies. I don't know what it will do, but if I had to guess I would say it's more dangerous than anything else on Earth."

"Why," Kayla said, her eyes slowly clearing as the adrenaline and the situation forced her to sober up a bit.

"Because there won't be anything human about it. The human element of the wolf has always been able to keep it in check to a point. Tyler even forced it to stop for a moment, which is something I've never heard of. But I don't think there would be anything human left in Doug to keep the wolf in check."

"What makes you think that?"

"He hasn't tried to contact any of you since his disappearance from the morgue. Is that like him?"

"Well no, but-" Amy began before Kayla interrupted.

"He came to see me again this morning. He looked in my window. I know it was him. He was pale and skinny, but I know his face. It was him."

"That's exactly what I'm afraid of," Jack said. "You believe he killed your dog the night after his body was found, and now you've seen his face twice. I think the wolf was drawn here, to you, because you are what Doug loved. It's been confused because the human feelings are so faint. Did he like your dog?"

"No. He hated her."

"Exactly. The wolf felt some emotion in relation to the dog so it killed her. Now it's biding its time trying to figure out how he felt about you. Have you gone outside at night lately?"

"Not since we found Tyler."

"Then I would say the only time it's seen your face is when it looked in your window. At least until just a few moments ago. The wolf can't be exposed to the sun for some reason. The moon is where it gets its power. It saw you after it had started to go dormant. If I had to guess I would say Doug's body has been laying in these woods during the day since the wolf escaped from the morgue, so the thing could rest."

"But that doesn't explain Tyler," Amy said.

"The wolf was in me. When I bit him on the blood moon it passed to him, freeing me."

"Then how did it get in Doug?"

"I think the wolf found him before he died. Tyler told me the police believed Doug had been partially eaten. I'm betting at least one bite got him before he died, spreading the curse. I think it filled him before he died and took him over slowly while he was in the morgue. It takes over on the third night, which is when they realized your boss was gone."

"How do we kill it?"

"I only know of two ways to destroy the wolf. It can either be killed by one who truly loves the person inside. Or it can be killed by another wolf."

"So I have to kill my Doug," Kayla said, her legs growing weak as she tried hard to be sober enough to understand the situation.

"No," Amy said. "Oh God. That's why he came here. Tyler is going to try to kill it."

"I'm afraid so," Jack said.

"This thing could tear him apart, couldn't it?

"In theory, the creature inside my son should be stronger, but if the wolf is the only thing left inside Doug's body, I have no idea what it's capable of."

"So," Kayla said, a moment of clarity bringing her to a sad understanding. "I need to kill Doug."

"Yes. Or we have to pray Tyler can."

"Is that Doug or Tyler outside," Amy asked, feeling overwhelmed herself, hoping she'd wake up any second and find it was all a dream.

"I'm thinking it was Doug. Tyler would likely be coming up the road, not from the woods."

"If Tyler does get the wolf here, how does he know it won't just kill you," Amy asked Jack.

"Why would it kill me?"

"You said it comes after the person its host loves most."

"Yes, Amy. And that person would be you."

Chills ran down her spine as the gaunt old man looked into her eyes. Some part of her had been wanting to hear that this may the case, while the rest of her couldn't be more terrified. Her heart fluttered at the thought Tyler loved her, more even than his own father, but her stomach churned at the thought that it may be that very love that would claim her life.

"Assuming it would come here for me, wouldn't Tyler know that? Why would he come here if I would be in danger?"

"He was able to stop it last night. It's why he sent me on ahead. If he can't direct the wolf and kill Doug, you have to kill him and make sure Kayla kills the other. I'll watch her if you'll watch for Tyler."

"Where did you leave him?"

"On the road just beyond where the wolf attacked him. Jasper stayed behind to make sure I got away."

"Jasper?"

"The dog. Buddy. He's mine."

Amy was speechless. Could this all really be happening? She looked at the guns in her hands, turning to Jack as the growling from outside picked up again.

"Which one is better?"

"If I'm right about what kills them, you're fine with the pistol. It doesn't matter what punch the gun has for me, if Kayla can't kill Doug my only goal is to keep you alive until Tyler gets here."

She tossed the shotgun to Jack, watching as he filled his pockets with shells and checked the gun. The empty box skittered across the floor as the first window broke. Doug raised the gun and watched as the dark shadow paused to peer inside before darting off to the left. Amy kept her gun trained on the door, putting her back against the nearest wall so she could brace herself against it. Fear filled the three of them, the scent floating to the nose of the wolf on the porch, making it snarl and growl in a way that almost sounded like it was trying to say Kayla's name. Jack told her she needed to be ready in case it came inside. She'd have to be the one to shoot it.

Jack leveled the gun at the window as the wolf stepped in front of it again. He could almost feel the power of the monster outside and knew it was worse than the thing he'd had inside of himself. The wolf outside had all of the cunning of a human and none of the emotional hang-ups. It was, he thought, the perfect killing machine, and he knew it wouldn't go down easy.

As he watched the wolf crouched low, the torn curtains billowing around its face in the wind. Jack could see the angry features twist as the spirit inside of Doug's body recognized him as its former host. Saliva ran down the thing's lolling tongue as it imagined the taste of Jack's flesh. The eyes that were locked on Jack's glowed a deep yellow as he examined the face they stared out of. Scars crisscrossed nearly every inch of skin, the deep black color of the stretched face broken up by bright white lines going in every direction. Looking farther out the window as the curtains blew around, Jack saw that the scars actually covered the thing's entire body. Large patches of skin were covered in thick white scar tissue, no hair growing in these places. He was particularly drawn to a large nest of scars that was situated where the wolf's neck met its shoulder. Jack instantly recognized that as the place where he'd bitten the dying man.

The wolf leaned slowly in the window, its eyes locked on Jack, freezing him in place. He finally shook himself out of his trance when he heard Amy say his name. Looking down he saw that the wolf had leaned far into the window, one paw braced on the bottom of the frame, and looked ready to launch itself inside the house. He didn't hesitate. He aimed for the thing's head and pulled the trigger, watching as blood, fur and bits of flesh flew everywhere. The face of the wolf virtually disintegrated, the force of the blow knocking it back out the window as mandible swung around, attached with little more than sinew, exposing a horror none of them had prepared for. The pallid face of Doug Morris looked out at them from a bleeding nest of flesh, gray skin covered in blood and fur as the wolf staggered. Jack ran to the window, cocked the shotgun, and blew another round into its abdomen, watching as the pellets ripped large holes in the wolf's flesh. It rolled to the side as he prepared to follow it out the window, finding the stairs and letting itself roll into the open air. Jack knew it would be healing in no time as it rolled into the moonlight. He put one leg on the window sill and braced himself, stopping when he heard Kayla say his name.

"Jack," she said, standing slowly. "Was that Doug? Was that his face … inside that beast?"

"I think so, Kayla," he said, turning to her slowly, unsure what to expect.

"It did, but it didn't look like Doug."

"It didn't?"

"The eyes I mean. I expected to see some little part of his looking back. But there wasn't. I think you're right. He's gone. That damn thing took him from me. You took him from me."

"Kayla, I didn't-"

"Stop," she said, interrupting him. "Just stop. I want to hear an explanation, but not now. All I know is that thing out there might be using Doug's body, but it ain't Doug. If I'm the one that has to kill it give me my gun."

Jack obliged, giving her two fresh shells when she moved to reload the weapon. She filled her pockets with as many shells as she could, Jack keeping the rest and promising to stay close in case she needed them. As they braced themselves and looked at the window again a low, mournful, pain filled howl rose from just beyond the porch. Jack felt the skin all over his body break out in goosebumps as he heard the sound grow louder, going on for much longer than any of them thought possible. Just as it reached its apex and began to lower and fade another joined it from not very far away. Tyler had reached the house at last.

***

Jack and Amy looked at each other as this new howl floated up the driveway on the breeze that blew the curtains inward. The wolf beside the porch leaped to its feet as Amy opened the door, Jack right behind her. It looked out at the new shadow bounding up the driveway and bared its fangs, snarling as the last of its flesh was healed, blood still dripping from its abdomen. Tyler leaped over the still running car and skidded to a halt in front of the darker wolf, roaring as he raised himself to a height that exceeded that of the scarred creature. Amy was frozen to the spot as she watched this spectacle, feeling she had suddenly been plunged into one of the nightmares she'd so recently told Tyler had no basis in reality. She felt Jack's large but gentle hand touch her shoulder and she felt confidence to step out onto the porch like she knew she shouldn't.

The two wolf creatures faced off in the driveway of Kayla's house, growling more fiercely than anything Amy had ever heard. The wolf that had taken over Doug's body was a smaller, squat creature, but it seemed to be ready to die for what it wanted just as much as Tyler. Amy watched as the broad backed, dark brown wolf that she knew resided in the body of the man she loved, circled the smaller one, its claws spread to show itself as a threat. She held her gun up slowly, ready to shoot if Tyler broke his concentration on the other animal. She watched as he stopped moving and hunched over, his legs tensing as he prepared for an attack. Without warning the other wolf dipped forward, its mouth closing around Tyler's forearm before ripping away a chunk of flesh. Tyler reacted like lightning, his right hand swinging around and catching the other wolf across the face, causing its right eye to burst as layers of flesh sagged with the newly opened wounds.

Jack watched in amazement as these wounds did not heal. He had never seen a fight between two wolves and wasn't sure what to expect. Tyler bounded forward and slashed at the other wolf's leg, catching it in the thigh before rolling to his feet. The wolf's leg buckled as the pain filled its body, causing a howl of pain as Tyler came in for another attack. He wasted no time as he slashed at the wolf from every direction before darting his head forward and trying to bite the wolf's throat. It pulled back at the last second, leaving Tyler's jaws to snap closed with enough force to make him blink his eyes a few times as he regained his composure. This was the window the wolf needed. It dove at Tyler, wrapping its arms around his waist and knocking him to the ground. It opened its jaws wide over his stomach, ready to gut him mercilessly.

Three shots rang out in the darkness, the bullets all catching the wolf in the head, throwing it off of Tyler and opening three large craters on the left side of its head. It lay there, the wounds all smoking as the moonlight went to work, as Tyler clambered to his feet and snapped his jaws closed over the thing's leg, shaking his head until they all heard the clear snap of bone breaking. Grabbing the leg in his hands, Tyler bit down hard, ripping the wolf's foot free of the leg as the thing screamed in an eerily human way. They all knew, as they watched blood gush from the wound, that they would never forget the sound as long as they lived. Tyler went in again, ready to take more of the wolf's leg, but was caught unawares by its other foot. He was knocked to the ground as the wolf brought its paw around and kicked him in the jaw, the sound seeming terrible from where Amy stood. She watched in horror as the wolf stood on its nub, pain causing it to emit a sound that ground its way into her brain and made her tremble in fear.

The wolf dug its claws into Tyler's back and picked him up in a frighteningly human way, launching his body at his car with enough force to shatter every window and make the vehicle rock upwards onto two wheels, dangerously close to turning over. He slid to the ground before the car dropped, falling in the exact spot the tires were going to land. They all heard the crunching grind of bones as the car fell onto Tyler's sternum and pelvis, feeling it was all over for their loved one. The scarred wolf turned to the house again, a leer of defiance on its face as it leaped from the yard to the porch in one bound. It had barely landed on the porch rails before a shotgun blast knocked it back into the yard, leaving the remains of its hand behind. It screamed in pain again as they watched it writhe in pain. No smoke rose from the wound as it held the stump of its wrist up in the moonlight, blood pouring from the wound. They watched as it rolled over and buried the stump of its hand in the loose dirt around the driveway, the blood caking the wound and staunching the flow of blood as it stood on one leg.

The sound of creaking springs filled the yard as Tyler lifted the car from his body and rolled out of the way. More glass rained down on the driveway as the car dropped back onto all four tires while Tyler raised himself to his feet. He launched himself at other wolf as smoke poured from his mouth. The wolf caught him in the air with its remaining hand and threw him sideways into a large tree. His body fell to the ground, smoke now rising from every inch of his skin as the wolf approached slowly. The mist began to clear as the wolf got close to him, revealing

Tyler, all signs of the wolf gone, lying unconscious at the base of the tree. Fresh growls rose from the wolf as it raised its claws to strike, Amy screamed once without being able to stop herself. Another gunshot rang out from the window as the wolf prepared to strike, the buckshot just grazing the ribs of the wolf before blowing a chunk of bark from the tree trunk.

The wolf dropped its hand instantly, turning to snarl at Kayla as she raised the gun and pointed it at the beast. Without hesitating it turned away and limped off into the trees, the sound of its growls fading away as they all rushed forward to get Tyler before it came back. Jack grabbed his son, lifting him up in arms that were surprisingly strong as Kayla stopped at the edge of the porch, bending to pick something up.

Jack turned, urging Amy and Kayla back into the house as he ran in and placed Tyler on the couch gently, checking for a pulse before backing away to join the women at the window.

"What if he turns again," Kayla said as she scanned the yard for movement.

"It shouldn't matter. The change will take long enough for us to get away."

Amy was speechless as she looked at the man she loved, now seeing the resemblance between father and son as tears rolled down her face. Jack placed a hand on her shoulder again, telling her she could go to him. It wouldn't be a problem. She hurried to the couch and dropped to her knees in front of him, covering his nakedness with a blanket before kissing his forehead. She felt his breathing as she rested her head on her hands, its rhythm no different than it was when he slept. She gripped her gun tightly as she knelt beside him, barely able to believe that he had been the other wolf in the yard. Her mind swam with the information she felt had been forced upon her in the last half hour. She'd woken up this morning believing monsters to be figments of an overactive child's imagination and now the man she loved had turned into a wolf. The idea was beyond anything she'd ever heard, and she began to laugh in spite of herself.

"What's funny," Jack said from the window.

"This. All of it. It can't be real. Monsters don't exist. Humans can't turn into wolves. It can't be real, but...but I've seen it. I know it is. If I can't rely on my own eyes what can I rely on?"

"It's real, alright," Kayla said sternly. "I've got the proof if you need it."

Amy stood as Jack questioned Kayla, his hand on the knife neither of them had realized he had until now. She reached into her pocket, and pulled out two small things that neither Jack nor Amy recognized at first. As Amy walked closer it hit her what they were. Kayla held two human fingers. Amy gasped involuntarily, quickly asking where Kayla had picked them.

"They were below the rail out there, right where I shot the wolf. I don't know if this means the thing is Doug or not, but it's obviously somehow a human, just like Tyler."

"Then what I thought is right," Jack said slowly. "It must be Doug. You shot him. He couldn't heal because the wound was made by you."

"Maybe it was just the gunshot itself," Kayla said, setting the fingers down on the windowsill and wiping her hands on her shirt.

"No, Amy shot it, too, remember? The wounds healed almost instantly."

Kayla said nothing, but turned her face to the yard once more, hoping Jack didn't notice the tears that spilled from her eyes. The trio watched over Tyler and the yard until the sky began to grow lighter. Jack felt his tension ease as he realized they had survived the night. He knew with Tyler already here, the other wolf severely wounded, and the three of them together they had a fighting chance at defeating the thing living in his son's former boss if it returned that night.

"I think we can relax a bit now," he said slowly, his ear ringing with the sound of his own voice after such a long silence.

"I would say so. It was around this time that I saw Doug looking at me yesterday, so I'd say he - it - is about to sleep. Unless it bled to death overnight," she said hopefully, looking to Jack to see if that was possible.

"I wouldn't bank on it. Do you want to fix this window before tonight or leave it as it is?"

"Will it do any good?"

"I don't know. It would take a very strong material to keep it out, but we could nail some plywood up."

"That would block a lot of visibility and an escape route, too," Kayla said. "We'll leave it open until this is over."

Jack agreed and asked what they would like to do with Tyler, glad to see that Amy had wrapped his wounded arm some time through the night.

"I guess he can have the guest bed for now," Kayla said, offering her own bed to Jack, knowing Amy wouldn't leave Tyler's side.

"I would rather stand watch down here if you don't mind," he said, "that is, if you trust me with the gun again."

"After this, I'll trust you to do surgery on me if it means I don't have to deal with that wolf right now."

Jack nodded and carried Tyler into the room Amy led him to, thanking her for taking care of his son before moving to leave them alone.

"Jack," she said, holding Tyler's hand as she sat on the bed with him.

"Yes, dear?"

"Why weren't you there for him? Growing up, I mean."

"His mother and I decided it was the best way to protect him from the wolf."

"She knew?"

"Oh yes. I didn't keep anything from Anna. I loved her - still love her - with all of my heart. Just like I do Tyler."

Jack walked out of the room and closed the door, leaving Amy to spend some time alone with the man she loved. She held his hand tightly as she replayed the events of the night before in her head again and dozing lightly, jerking herself awake when she heard Tyler say her name.

"Amy," he said, squinting in the light of the sun streaming through the window.

"Hey there, hero," she said with a smile, kissing his head again as she got up to close the blinds.

"Please tell me it worked."

"Sort of."

"What do you mean," he said, sitting up slowly, wincing when he put pressure on his injured arm.

"Well, you got him good, so did Kayla, but he ran off into the woods. Kayla hopes he might bleed to death. But if not, we'll all be here to take care of him."

"No. You can't be here. The two of you have to leave. Leave Doug to me. I can take care of it."

"If we leave he won't come back here. He'll follow us. It's Kayla he's after, remember?"

"Partially. But I don't think he'll go anywhere until he takes care of someone else first."

"Who?"

"My father."

"What are you talking about," Amy asked after staring at him for a moment.

"If the wolf in Doug's body feels anything like the one in mine does, it wants Dad dead almost as much as it wants to taste Kayla's flesh. It could sense Dad was near no matter what was going on. It could smell him. If the other wolf hadn't been there, or hadn't knocked me out, I think I might have attacked him myself."

"Oh. Do you think he knows?"

"I doubt it. He killed his own father, so I would assume he never felt the wolf's hatred for the one who passed it on. Then again, he also had to watch as the wolf ate part of the man's body, so he may well have an idea. What the hell is up with my arm," he asked as he put pressure on it again only to have it give out under him. "I thought I could heal from anything."

"Apparently not. Did Jack tell you that a loved one could kill a wolf?"

"Yeah, and so can another wolf."

"Yes. Well apparently those two wounds don't heal very well, either. Which is good."

"How is this good?"

"Not your arm, but you bit one of the other wolf's feet off. And you scratched its face to ribbons. And Kayla shot its hand off."

"So she may be right. If it does bleed to death we're done. But if it doesn't, then it'll come back that much more angry. And, knowing what I know, I wouldn't be surprised if it came with a plan."

The two sat in silence for a few moments before Tyler wrapped his arm around Amy and drew her in close, hugging her tightly. She could feel that he had gotten so much stronger since the attack, his hug seeming tight enough to crack bones, but she loved it. She felt secure as he held her to his body. Slowly she reached up and traced the line of his large bicep with her finger, feeling that, even though she could be in imminent danger, she had made the right choice about the man beside her. She leaned up and kissed him softly, running her tongue in his mouth when he didn't pull back. She felt her heart rate quicken as she became aroused. The danger and fear from the night before melted away as she let him pull her clothes off. She felt him growing hard under the sheet and pulled it off, getting ready to be with him again, her body wanting him more than ever.

The two felt the rise and fall of their bodies in a way they hadn't imagined before the change, Tyler's muscles moving in ways they didn't before. They did their best to stay quiet while they made love, but the experience was even better than it had been before and by the time they were done they felt sure at least one of the other two people in the house had heard them. Amy laid her head on Tyler's chest, catching her breath before rolling over and laying on her side, leaning on her arm to talk to him.

"Tyler?"

"Yeah, honey," he said, feeling his stomach churn with a hunger that he was unwilling to admit.

"When this is over … what do we do?"

"What do you mean?"

"I mean when Doug is taken care of. When you're you again tomorrow. Where do we go from here?"

"I don't know, actually. I guess I'll have to talk to Dad about it all."

"What can Jack tell you?"

"How to handle it. How to live with it. I already surprised him. Maybe I can get it under control."

"Surprised him?"

"Yeah. With the wolf. The first time I turned."

"How?"

"I was able to stop it. I made it listen to me. I took control back, basically."

"Did he never do that?"

"Actually he told me he's never heard of anyone doing it."

Amy pondered on this information while she listened to Tyler's stomach continue to growl. They kissed again and Amy dressed herself, Tyler finding an old pair of sweatpants to cover himself until nightfall. They walked downstairs together and found his father lying on the couch with the shotgun across his chest, dozing lightly. They walked into the room to wake Jack up and found a surprise waiting for them as they crossed the threshold of the room. A dark brown lump lay on the floor in front of Jack, moving as it heard the floorboards creak. Tyler gasped audibly when the black tail began to wag, Jasper stretching before limping over to them on a leg that was slightly swollen. Tyler hugged Jasper as he was greeted with licks and panting.

"He came in about an hour after you went up," Jack said, propping the gun against the arm of the couch and standing to stretch. "I imagine you're starving."

"More than I care to admit," Tyler said sheepishly, his stomach growling loudly again.

"Let's go see what Kayla has in her kitchen," Amy said. "I don't think she'll mind."

They walked in and found a large pack of steaks as well as some hamburger meat in the refrigerator, deciding this would do. Amy went up to make sure Kayla was OK and to see if she would join them, leaving father and son alone.

"Dad, what am I supposed to do?"

"About Amy?"

"Yeah. She asked me what our next step was, and I honestly have no idea."

"Do you love each other?"

"Of course."

"Then you'll find the answer together, just like your mother and I did."

"But you and Mom hate each other."

"No we don't. We hate our situation. I can't be near her, couldn't be near you as long as the wolf was in me."

"Did she know that was the reason you stayed gone?"

"Oh yes. She knew from the beginning. I never lied to your mother. I told her about my condition as soon as I was able to fully realize it was real. I shared everything with her."

"And she still married you?"

"Of course. Tyler, your mother and I were in love. To me we still are. I see the same thing between you and Amy. The two of you can figure this out, whatever it takes. If you want to be together, nothing will stop you."

"But what about kids? I can't risk passing this on to my child. Dad, I can't do that. "

Jack looked at the floor, knowing that he had said those exact words to his wife before they were married. "Tyler, I don't know what to tell you about that. I thought our plan would work. I left and looked for a cure every time a full moon was coming. For thirty years I've tried to find a way to reverse it."

"Have you been able to find anything?"

"Rumors. Crap mostly. I've tried all of it. Except for one thing."

"What?"

"In Ireland I came across an old woman in a village who recognized the condition instantly. She told me the only way to cure the curse is to cut it off at the source. She said the curse can be ended if one who has been cursed takes the life of the one who gave it to them."

"What the hell?"

"That's what she said. It has to be while you're in control, not the wolf."

"So in order for you to be cured, you would have had to kill your father."

"Basically. It has to happen after the curse takes over, after your first turn and while you're human. The wolf killing them is just another murder."

"But doesn't everyone die when they pass it?"

"Everyone has before. I think that's why. The wolf knows that's its weakness so it makes sure there is no chance of a cure."

"But, you're alive."

"I am."

"Then why are you telling me this?"

"You're my son. I did this to you. If there is a chance it could work..."

"No. Dad, I couldn't if I wanted to. You're my father."

"But if it works..."

"If it doesn't then I just murdered my father. The odds aren't worth it. There must be something else."

"The other thing she said made no sense."

"What was it," Tyler demanded as his stomach continued to churn and rumble.

"She said if you end the curse where it began it will free everyone afflicted."

"What does that mean?"

"Generally, I think it is more a cure for a short-term attack. If you kill the first person who had the curse, everyone they've cursed will be cured."

The pair grew silent as they heard a set of footsteps coming down the stairs toward the kitchen. Amy popped around the corner with a smirk on her face.

"Kayla said she wanted to sleep, but we are welcome to eat anything we want."

"What's so funny," Tyler said, putting on his best fake smile.

"She told me to let you know that if you pee on her carpet she'll rub your nose in it no matter how big you get."

The three shared a nervous laugh as they put the steaks on the stove to cook with a few slices of the pepper they found in a basket on the counter. Tyler stepped outside, hoping Amy didn't see what was in his hand. Jasper followed him out the door, the two of them walking around the house and out of sight while Jack kept Amy distracted with small talk. When they were safely out of sight Tyler unwrapped the hamburger and threw a piece to Jasper before taking a bite of the cold, raw meat. He was instantly elated by the taste filling his mouth. He felt the wolf inside of him calming as he swallowed the bloody beef. He took bite after bite, Jasper circling his feet to pick up the crumbs that hit the ground, and before he knew it there was none left. He belched loudly after swallowing the last of the meat and threw the wrapper in the bushes to keep from having to admit that he had done such a thing. He knelt down and wiped his mouth on the dark sweatpants, finding himself much more flexible than normal, and vaulted up when the scent of fresh cooked steak hit his nostrils. He jogged back to the house and into the door as his father was removing one steak from the heat.

"We thought you'd probably want yours rare," Jack said, a slight amount of pity - or was it envy - in his voice.

Tyler thanked them both and sat down at the table, cutting one bite of the meat before he made himself wait on the others. The blood from the steak ran down his throat as he chewed, the juicy cut of beef squishing between his teeth in a way that strangely reminded him of the bear the wolf had killed on his first change. Amy and Jack sat down at the table a few minutes later, both kindly averting their eyes as Tyler sliced chunk after chunk of meat from his steak. He felt the beast inside of him finally begin to rest as he got to the end of the meat, realizing as he finished that they had given him the largest piece.

"That was great, Dad," he said when he was finished, wiping his mouth slowly, keeping his eyes upward so he wouldn't see the blood on the plate, knowing he wouldn't be able to prevent himself from drinking it.

"I've had plenty of practice," he said ambiguously. "I'm glad you enjoyed it. Amy, is yours OK?"

"It's great. These peppers really work with it."

The afternoon passed slowly as the three of them sat around, occasionally walking to the porch or telling a joke. Tyler asked his father to talk about his life as the evening drew on. He could already feel the wolf awakening. His mind tried to fill with rage every time he heard his father's voice, but he fought it, suppressing it after a few attempts. They heard Kayla come down the stairs and sit at the foot of them. Tyler could smell the salt in her tears. The sun sank lower as they talked, Jack talking of his life trying to run from the wolf, knowing that sooner or later he would be overtaken. Tyler felt the wolf rise once, just as the sun went behind the trees outside, a growl escaping his throat before he pushed the urge back down.

"What happened," Amy said, sliding over as Jack pulled the shotgun out of Tyler's reach.

"It's trying to rise. It's almost like it wants to get in my head instead of take over my body."

"Why," Kayla said, walking in and handing Amy the gun none of them knew she'd grabbed.

"It's Dad. It really hates Dad."

"That doesn't surprise me. That's probably why the wolf always sees to the death of its former host. It's all about self-preservation. I think we all realized that last night."

"Oh yeah. I think it's even worse after Doug bested it."

"Son, whether you want to admit it or not, there is nothing left of Doug in that creature. You can tell that by looking at it."

"What do you mean?"

"Do you remember seeing it?"

"Yeah. It was actually kind of smallish, and scarred."

"Exactly. I think Doug's body died even before the wolf could heal it. It's literally living with Doug's body in the exact shape it was in when he died. To be honest, that may be our main advantage."

"How so?"

"Because, unlike you, it has no human element, remember. It doesn't have a human conscience on any level, I don't think. It's pure animal. That's why it seems so fierce."

"In all honesty, Dad, you were pretty fierce too."

"I'm aware. Now, we need to prepare. You have to tell us when it comes up again."

"I can't let it out while you're here."

"You'll have to. There is no time to wait. When it wants to come you have to let it. We can't risk you being in mid-change when the other one comes."

"Can't you all hold it off it that is the case?"

"We could try, but once you finished turning you'd come after us if it was already taken care of."

"I don't want to hurt any of you."

"There is still another option."

"I can't do that, Dad. You know that. It might not even work."

"Do what," Amy interjected, making sure her gun was fully loaded.

"Kill me," Jack said matter-of-factly.

"What?!"

"He thinks killing him would take the curse away. Some crazy old witch doctor told him it might work."

"Jack, he's right. You're his father. What would it do to him if he killed you? If it does work then, yes he'll be free, but either way he would always have to live knowing that he killed his own father. No, I wouldn't let him if he wanted to," Amy said sternly. "It isn't an option."

"Fine. Tyler, you need to be ready. Go to the porch and give them time to hide."

"I'm not leaving him," Amy said, a single tear running down her cheek.

"You have to Amy," Tyler said, taking her in his arms and kissing her passionately. "But first I need you to do something."

"Don't-" she started.

"I need you to promise me that you'll do whatever it takes to keep yourself safe. I don't care if you have to kill me. I'd rather be dead than live knowing I killed you."

"You think I wouldn't?"

"Amy please. I need this. You have to promise me."

"Tyler-"

"Promise!"

"Fine," she shouted as she began to sob. "Fine. I'll do it. Just please, please don't make me. Don't make do it."

"I'll do my best. I love you, Amy."

"I love you, too. Please come back to me."

They kissed again, Tyler stepping out of the broken window as his stomach cramped again. He could see the moon rising over the mountains, its silky light falling through the rails of the porch and landing on his legs. He removed his pants as the cramp hit him again, making him drop to his knees. He heard Jasper leap out onto the porch to put himself between Tyler and Jack, and felt thankful that the dog's growling partially blocked the sound of Amy and Kayla running around in the house behind him. He felt the first muscle spasms in his back and legs as he heard the sound that made his blood run cold. From behind the house came one long, low mournful howl.

"Oh shit," Jack said from inside, checking the shotgun as Amy screamed.

"He's not ready," she said, fighting Kayla as she ran to the front room and leveled her gun at the shadow of her slowly changing boyfriend.

"This isn't going to be pretty," Jack warned. "You might want to turn away."

"I won't leave him defenseless."

"I'm here. So is Jasper."

"I can't, Jack. I love him. Anna wouldn't leave you, would she?"

"No," he said, sadly. "She never would."

Tyler felt the wolf inside of him wake up and begin fighting to emerge as another howl rang into the night, this one from the right side of the house, growing slowly closer. He felt his bones snap and grind together as they reformed. He realized the process was going faster than before and felt hopeful that he would be ready when the other wolf reached him. His arms and hands changed before his eyes, his fingers stretching slowly as claws sprouted from the ends of them, the bones in his back twisting and bending slightly. The bandage fell off of his wounded arm, revealing a red, oozing chunk of missing flesh that stung in the fresh air. He heard footsteps from beside the porch as he stood on newly formed legs, his face slowly changing. He chanced one look through the window and saw Amy's face, terrified and tear streaked looking back at him.

He roared as his mandible broke, his pallet extending forward to create a protruding snout, his eyes repositioning themselves as he turned to focus on the threat that approached him cautiously. The wolf limped forward, one leg little more than a muddy, oozing stump, holding an arm that was the same. It kept its head slightly turned so it could focus on him with its remaining eye, its lips pulled back to reveal yellow, blood stained teeth. He stretched his claws and jumped over the railing, landing in front of the wolf, lashing out with his claws the second he landed.

The wolf inside of Tyler wasted no time once it made contact with the other. Blood poured as slash after slash opened on the already injured wolf's body. It seemed to bide its time, letting him slash at it until he hesitated for a second. It took that opportunity to pounce. Tyler was thrown off balance and landed on the ground with the surprisingly heavy wolf on top of him. Screams broke out from inside the house as the wolf grabbed his face with its remaining hand, squeezing and pushing his head aside to expose his neck. Tyler roared in rage and tried to throw the other wolf off of his chest. He panicked as the wolf inside him was unable to fight off the enemy, taking over and jabbing his claws into the thing's back, eliciting a howl of pain unlike anything he'd ever heard. He pushed his fingers in further as he felt the wolf squeeze his face harder. He felt the warm, wet form of the wolf's spine pass his fingers and got an idea. He pushed harder and closed his fingers, digging his claws through flesh and muscle to wrap his fingers around the spine of the wolf. It lifted his head and slammed him into the ground as it snarled in fresh pain. He felt the world begin to fade as the pressure grew to be too much.

Blackness crept in at the edge of his vision as he tried to find the strength to break the wolf's back. He was losing his grip on reality, the wolf fighting like mad within him when something hit the wolf from the side, making it lose its grip on his head. He instantly felt reality come back, his vision returning as the wolf's spine was ripped from his grip. He rolled to his feet, watching as the wolf rolled around with a fierce ball of black and brown fur. Smoke filled the air as the dog caused wound after wound to the wolf, sustaining just as many himself. The wolf inside of Tyler regained composure and instantly felt hatred at the dog for interrupting his fight. Tyler watched as the creature inside him pushed his body forward, grabbing the other wolf by the leg and jerking it towards him, leaving Jasper a bloody lump in the yard.

The wolf growled at him as it regained its bearings. Tyler felt his fist slam into the ribs of the wolf on the ground and relished in the sound of ribs cracking. The wolf sank its teeth into his leg, making him lose his balance. It opened its mouth and grabbed his tail as he fell down, bringing itself onto his back and pushing his face into the ground. It snarled loudly and sank its teeth into the back of his neck. He was unable to move as the pressure on his neck built until he could feel the vertebrae being strained. He faintly heard the sounds of screaming and gunshots coming closer as he tried to push himself up. Shotgun blasts sounded right over his head as his breath hitched in his chest. He felt the wolf scream against his neck as gunshot after gunshot wracked its body. Finally he felt it let go, giving him a chance to roll over and see what had made the wolf hesitate.

Tyler saw with relief that his father was standing over the body of the wolf, cocking the shotgun and pumping more rounds into its head. Smoke raised slowly as the moonlight allowed the wolf to heal. Tyler felt the wolf inside of him recognize his father, tried to stop it from moving and tried to warn his father. He was only able to emit a large growl, turning his father's attention to him. Jack raised the shotgun as the wolf took control of Tyler again, launching his body through the air. Jack tried to pull the trigger, getting the shot off at the last second, only grazing Tyler's shoulder as the wolf slammed into his body. Claws pierced Jack's shoulders as the heavy wolf pinned him to the ground, sinking its teeth into his neck and ripping his head from his body before Tyler had a chance to stop it. He screamed as he tasted his father's flesh. The wolf lost control as he felt his own anger rise. He opened his mouth and screamed as the wolf behind him snarled in anger, its wounds almost healed. Tyler, still in control, turned quickly and reached out, grabbing the wolf by the throat and lifting it high above his head.

He watched the wolf writhe in pain as his claws dug deeper and deeper into its neck. It kicked its good leg up at him, trying to catch hold enough to allow it to pull away. Without thinking he grabbed the wolf's leg and snapped it, relishing in the scream of pain that filled the air. He twisted the broken leg in his land as the wolf struggled, lashing out with its good hand. It caught him right behind the ear with its claws and dug in. He howled in anger and pain as the wolf inside of him struggled to regain control. He fought it back as he continued fighting with the wolf in his hand. In one swift motion he ripped the flesh from the wolf's broken leg as it closed its hand around his ear and pulled. He felt his skin tear, his ear and what felt like half of his face came free in the wolf's hand. Tyler felt his tongue slide sideways and dangle between his now-exposed teeth. The wolf dropped the bloody hunk of his flesh as Amy screamed again in the background.

Tyler dropped the wolf to the ground as the pain of his wound set in, hesitating enough for the wolf inside of him to take control again. He watched as the wolf looked down at the pitiful creature now writhing on the ground. He felt his foot raise and stomp on the newly broken leg of the wolf, satisfaction rising in him as he stomped down again. The wolf was taken aback when a gunshot rang out, buckshot taking him by surprise and blowing him forward and to his knees. Tyler shook his head against the fresh pain, watching in horror as he turned around to see Kayla running down the front stairs, shotgun at the ready.

"Leave him alone," she yelled, tears in her eyes. "Kill him quick, you don't have to torture him.

Tyler tried to take control again as the wolf snarled at Kayla, watching in horror as Amy ran down the stairs behind her. He felt the wolf lurch forward against his will, the mangled creature on the ground grabbing at his tail to try and pull him down. Kayla stopped a few feet away and brought her gun up quickly, blasting off a shot before the wolf could react. Tyler felt the other half of his face explode in a nest of pain, his vision blurring as his right eye was obliterated. The blast blew him off his feet, landing him in the reach of the other wolf as he heard Amy scream his name. He waited for the wolf to climb on top of him and finish its work, but to his surprise he felt it move away. As his vision slowly returned to normal, the itching sensation of the moonlight healing his wounds filling his subconscious, he realized it had to be going after what it had wanted all along.

As if to confirm his assumption Kayla let out a frightened yelp before the sound of growling filled the night. He heard gunshots and Amy begging for something to end. He rolled to his side as quickly as he could, watching as the wolf in front of him pulled Kayla to the ground and sank its teeth into her shoulder. He heard the crunch of bones as the wolf's hand clawed fresh chasms into her chest, her blood spilling onto the ground and soaking the wolf. Tyler pushed hard, taking control from the monster inside of him and reached out, grabbing the wolf by the stump of leg closest to him and squeezed. The wolf let Kayla go as it screamed in agony and turned on him. He wasted no time leaping to his feet and grabbing the other wolf by the head. He felt its claws rake his thigh as he lifted it high, holding it behind the ears and squeezing with all his might, feeling the skull in his hand begin to give slightly.

The next two things happened so fast he barely felt he had time to register them in his mind. He felt the wolf's claws pierce his stomach, the razor sharp nails slicing his skin and spilling his blood at an all new level. Upon feeling this his instant reaction was to both squeeze tighter and grab the wolf's lower jaw. The top of the wolf's head collapsed in his hand, a surge of blood, bone and brains rushing down his wrist and forearm while he pulled the mandible down, ripping the dead creature's head in two much as he had the bear's two nights before. Amy screamed again as this happened, making him turn towards her as he realized the threat was now eliminated. Kayla lay in a puddle of blood, her shoulder shredded to the bone and her sternum gleaming white in the moonlight. Tyler heard her struggling for breath as he surveyed the situation, realizing at the last second that everything could go very wrong.

Amy ran to Kayla, looking down at her friend before realizing she was only feet away from a creature that could do her the same way. Tyler felt the wolf surge forward and take control as it sensed Amy's connection to him. She raised her gun as the wolf took a step forward, silently begging for Tyler to be able to stop it. He felt the wolf's rage and hatred culminate as it looked at Amy. She could see the struggle within the beast as it moved toward her, its movements jerky and halting. The wolf tried to leap at Amy time and time again, but Tyler held on with all his might. He felt the creature raising his hands, opening and closing them, threatening to use the razor sharp claws that had already done so much damage.

Tyler watched as Amy backed all the way to the stairs, her gun pointed right at his chest, tears streaming down her face. The wolf saw that she was trapped and tried as hard as it could to break free and take her for its own. Tyler pushed as hard as he could, his mind straining with the effort to take over his body and keep the wolf from taking Amy. He didn't know how long he could hold the beast or how he could let her know it was OK, but he would have to try something. He struggled more and more as he felt the wolf crouch, ready to pounce. He could see Amy crying, hear her begging him to fix it, to save them both. He put forth as much effort as he had, feeling himself start to break, and felt a malicious streak course through his body.

In an instant the wolf pulled back, giving Tyler full control. He was trying so hard to gain his body back that the sudden change threw him off balance, sending him careening toward Amy. She reacted instinctively, pulling her trigger three times, shooting Tyler point blank in the chest. He felt the bullets from the high caliber handgun tear through his body as he stopped in his tracks, falling to his knees. He felt his heart throbbing extra hard, trying to make up for the fact that one side of the muscle had been shredded by a bullet. He let his body down easily as he saw his fingers shrinking back to their normal size, a light mist rising from his skin as he reverted back to his human form. He heard Amy sobbing behind him and rolled over so he could look up at her. He felt his face returning back to what it was, his body growing cold as the wind blew over his naked, blood soaked skin.

He turned his eyes up to Amy as the nest of pain in his chest became increasingly more oppressive. She dropped to her knees beside him, picking his head up and resting it in her lap after dropping her gun. Tears poured down her cheeks and fell onto Tyler's face, a sensation that brought him comfort as he realized the feeling was leaving his extremities. He took a deep breath and tried to speak to her.

"Amy," he wheezed, feeling his punctured lung more than ever. "You did the right thing."

"How can you say that? I've killed you. Oh my God, I've killed you."

Tyler took another deep breath as Amy began to grow hysterical. "You had to. The wolf...wanted you," He was interrupted by a violent, hacking cough, spraying blood into the air as he cried out in pain.

"Please forgive me. I'm so sorry, Tyler. I'm sorry."

"Amy, you saved me," he wheezed, feeling his life leave his body, his vision growing dark. "I love you. So much. Please....thank you...."

Amy screamed as she watched Tyler take his last breath, she watched as foamy, white blood poured from his mouth as his life left his body and whispered that she loved him, too. She wasn't sure how long she sat on the ground holding his body, rocking back and forth as she sobbed into the night.

"I'm sorry Amy," came a voice from beside her as she noticed the night growing lighter.

She looked up with a gasp, shocked to see Kayla standing in front of her, her body completely healed as her shredded clothes hung from her body. Amy had been sure Kayla would be dead after the wounds she'd sustained, yet here stood her friend, looking better than ever. What could that mean? She had, for just a moment, believed that this was over, but now, as Kayla asked her what happened, she wasn't so sure.

"You were attacked. Don't you remember?"

"No. The last thing I remember was that I shot him," she said, guiltily gesturing at Tyler's body. "And now I'll never get to say I'm sorry."

"He knew. He had to. He did this for us, Kay," she said, knowing she had to warn Kayla of what was coming. "You need to know something."

"Please. Tell me anything."

"You were bitten."

"I figured as much," Kayla said, gesturing to her tattered clothing. "But I don't seem to be hurt. Maybe the blood is Doug's?"

"No, honey. When the wounds heal like that.... I think it means the curse has passed."

"So this...I'm going to be one of them?"

"I think so, honey. I'm sorry."

Kayla said nothing as she sat on the stairs beside of her friend, the two of them watching the sun rise on the massacre in the yard, smiling as a familiar face slowly made its way to them, the horrors of the night slipping into a memory neither of them would ever be able to forget.

Epilogue

Amy sat on the front porch of her house, looking out at the view of the stars. She took a large gulp of warm cocoa to protect her from the still cool air. The last month had been fortunately mild, allowing her to find a job in the city and have some closure from her time with Tyler. She reached over and absentmindedly stroked Jasper's head, feeling the still healing scabs on his skin didn't seem to be raised so high anymore. She threw her hand up as a car drove past the house, its headlights illuminating the porch for just a moment before receding back into the darkness.

Amy watched the moon rise through the thin fog of the late winter evening as she finished her cocoa. Without warning the sound of a long, low, mournful howl split the night. As if this had been what was waiting for, Amy pushed herself up off the bench, calling for the dog as she shut and locked the door behind them, grabbing her gun for safety's sake.

Afterword

I would like to thank each and every one of you for joining me on this journey. The original version of this novel was written in less than three weeks. I spent countless hours every day inside this world I was creating, putting aside nearly every other aspect of my life to finish telling Tyler's tale. Since then I've gone through a few different edits, making improvements everywhere I could, trying to make his story the best it could be. What started as a cut and dry, one book tale became something I can't even predict. As you're reading this I am working on developing a potential sequel that will, hopefully, build on the tale of werewolves and their mountain haunts.

If you liked this book and you'd like to read more of my work, feel free to look for my short story and poetry collection *Tales of the Mysterious and the Macabre: Stories from the Appalachian Foothills,* available in print or eBook format. Check out my website, blog, social media presence, and all available purchases and updates on my writing at my website https://dameanmathews.com/. Thank you again for your undying support! You are all amazing!